DRIVE ME CRAZY

ROAD TRIPPING SERIES

SAMANTHA CHASE

DRIVE ME
Crazy

PRAISE FOR SAMANTHA CHASE

"If you can't get enough of stories that get inside your heart and soul and stay there long after you've read the last page, then Samantha Chase is for you!"

-*NY Times & USA Today Bestselling Author* **Melanie Shawn**

"A fun, flirty, sweet romance filled with romance and character growth and a perfect happily ever after."

-*NY Times & USA Today Bestselling Author* **Carly Phillips**

"Samantha Chase writes my kind of happily ever after!"

-*NY Times & USA Today Bestselling Author* **Erin Nicholas**

"The openness between the lovers is refreshing, and their interactions are a balanced blend of sweet and spice. The planets may not have aligned, but the elements of this winning romance are definitely in sync."

- *Publishers Weekly, STARRED review*

"A true romantic delight, *A Sky Full of Stars* is one of the top gems of romance this year."

- *Night Owl Reviews, TOP PICK*

"Great writing, a winsome ensemble, and the perfect blend of heart and sass."

As FAR AS wedding days went, Grace Mackie could say with great certainty that this one completely sucked.

And considering she was the bride, that was saying something.

Sitting alone in the bride's dressing room in the exclusive Lake Tahoe resort where her fiancé had *insisted* they have their destination wedding, she felt bored and oddly disappointed. This wasn't the wedding she had always dreamed of. As a matter of fact, it wasn't even the wedding she had planned.

Two weeks ago, Jared suggested the idea of eloping and no matter how much Grace resisted, he steamrolled ahead and now...here they were. Granted, the resort was the most luxurious she'd ever stayed at; her gown was amazing, and... even though California isn't exactly the destination that came to mind when she thought of destination weddings, it certainly didn't suck.

The downside was that they went from a big, family-filled wedding to a small and intimate event that most of her family and friends couldn't afford to attend. She had argued that point–among others–with Jared, but he had promised they'd have a big party when they got back to North Carolina. Getting married in Tahoe was a dream of his so she figured it wouldn't be so bad.

Except it was.

She was alone in this gorgeous dressing room and wished her best friend Lori or even her parents were here with her. A light knock at the door had her turning.

"Hey, Gracie! Thirty minutes until showtime! Are you ready?" The super-perky and extremely annoying wedding planner, Tilly, said with a smile as she walked through the door.

Smiling serenely, Grace replied, "Yes, thank you." Smoothing her hand down the white satin gown she was wearing, she tried to present the perfect image of the calm and serene bride-to-be.

Even though internally, she was like a squirrel in traffic.

"Great! In about twenty minutes, I'll come back and..."

"Tilly," Grace quickly interrupted before she could go any further. "If it's all right with you, we've gone over the schedule dozens of times and I'd really appreciate a few minutes to myself."

Tilly, with her severe bun and power suit, nodded. "Of course, Gracie. Anything you need," she smiled broadly and made her way back out the door, gently closing it behind her. At the sound of the soft click, Grace sagged with relief.

She hated being called Gracie. No one she knew *ever* called her Gracie. And yet for some reason, Tilly insisted on calling her that.

Catching a glimpse of herself in the full-length mirror, she should have been a happy and smiling bride. But was she? No. Instead, she was a neurotic mess who was dealing with more than your run-of-the-mill wedding jitters. She was angry, disappointed, and she knew if she didn't speak up for herself one last time, this was the way her entire marriage was going to go—with Jared making decisions she hated and then being resentful forever.

Knowing she wasn't going to breathe easy until she talked to him, Grace decided to go find him and hash this out. If it meant calling off the wedding, then so be it. It wasn't like she had any real investment in it. None of her family were here, Jared had made all the arrangements, and she had very little input into any of it.

Suddenly all the signs she should have seen were right there in front of her.

She was going to find Jared, tell him how she felt, and maybe they could look into couples counseling or something. It would be a good thing. It would help them grow closer. Looking back now, she realized this was a pattern that had gotten completely out of control. Why hadn't she noticed it sooner?

"Hindsight and all," she muttered, opening the door and stepping out into the hallway. They had toured the resort yesterday and she knew where the groom's dressing room was, so there was no need to ask for assistance from perky Tilly. At the end of the hall, she turned to the left and saw the door to Jared's room was ajar. The closer she got, Grace could hear him talking. Was Tilly giving him the thirty-minute speech too?

"You have to trust me, baby. It's all going to be okay. This is only temporary," she heard Jared saying.

Temporary? What was temporary?

"How could you do this, Jared? You said you loved me! You said we were going to be a family!"

What?!

Slowly, Grace moved closer to the door and tried to figure out who Jared was speaking to.

"We will, baby. We will," he promised. "You have to trust me, Steph. Marrying Grace will help me secure this promotion, and then six months from now, I'll divorce her and we'll be together. Just in time for the baby to be born."

Steph? *Steph?* Wait...the only Steph she knew was Jared's assistant, and he wouldn't...

"How am I supposed to come into work every day knowing you're sleeping with her every night?" Steph cried.

Grace heard Jared's soft laugh. "Baby, you need to relax. Grace and I haven't slept together for almost two months. What's a few more?"

Grace was about to barge through the door and put a stop to this, but...

"Just because she was stupid enough to fall for that whole 'wanting to make the wedding night sex better' excuse before doesn't mean she'll keep falling for it, Jared. And besides, tonight is your wedding night!"

"Don't worry," he cooed. "I'll come up with an excuse. The only woman I plan on sleeping with from now on is you."

Rage filled her, followed by a wave of nausea. How could she have been so blind? When Jared had mentioned not having sex to enhance their wedding night, it sounded kind of sexy. Hell, she had been horny all this time, and for what?

Taking several deep breaths, she told herself to calm down. Everything would be all right. She'd get through this. And then, something weird happened. She was suddenly calm–like eerily calm. It was true that Jared needed her to secure his promotion–Grace had been grooming him for the position of junior vice president of operations practically since they met! Her job as a career coach meant it was her specialty and Jared had begged her to help him move up in the company. She'd helped him change his image and his wardrobe and gave him lessons in manners and how to present himself in social situations. He was a complete doofus when she met him! And now that she transformed him, someone *else* was going to reap all the benefits of her hard work?

Well, she had news for him...he was *never* going to pull it off without her. He had definitely made great strides and his bosses were impressed, but without her there beside him, there was no way he was going to secure that promotion. His bosses weren't completely wowed by him yet and she had no intention of sticking around and helping him any longer. True, she could marry him and when he asked for a divorce, take him for everything he was worth, but that wasn't her style.

Wait, do I even have a style? She wondered.

Turning around, she made her way back toward her room and calmly walked inside and closed the door. In the corner was the small satchel that had her makeup bag, her wallet, her iPod and earbuds, her phone, and...

Before she knew it, the bag was in her hand and she was walking back out the door. The hallway was still deserted as she made her way to the rear exit and stepped outside. The sun was going down–Jared had said a sunset wedding would be romantic–and as she looked out at the lake, she had to admit the view would have been stunning.

"No time for that, dummy," she muttered, pulling her phone out of her bag and quickly pulling up the Uber app to request a ride. Saying a silent prayer that she wouldn't have to wait too long and risk someone finding her, she sagged with relief when the app showed a car was only five minutes away. Doing her best to stay out of sight, Grace hid behind some tall shrubs and prayed no one would come out and find her. Of course, a woman in a blindingly white gown didn't exactly blend into the greenery.

If they weren't so close to the ceremony time, she would have run up to their room and grabbed her luggage. Unfortunately, she didn't want to draw any attention to herself and would just have to deal with making her escape in her gown.

Staring at her phone, she willed the damn car to hurry up. The ride to the airport would take an hour, and she was hoping to get enough of a head start that should Jared try to come find her, she'd be on a plane before he could reach her.

Wishful thinking, but still...

Behind her, someone came out the back door but luckily, it was a janitor and he didn't even look in her direction. Her heart was beating a million miles an hour and when she glanced down at her phone again, she saw the car was two minutes out.

In any other circumstances, she would be pacing. Unfortunately, that wasn't an option right now and she suddenly wished she had packed a change of clothes in her satchel. If she were in jeans and sneakers, she would be trekking toward the road to meet up with the car and burning off some of this nervous energy. But no, she was stuck in this stupid, bulky gown hiding behind a shrub.

"Worst wedding day ever."

Seriously, in the history of wedding days, this one had to set some kind of new record in awfulness.

Off in the distance, Grace saw a car pulling into the resort driveway and was relieved when she realized it was her ride. Sprinting as well as she could from the bushes, she rushed to meet it and quickly jumped in.

"Are you Grace?" the driver asked.

"I am, I am," she said quickly. "Just drive. Please!" He looked at her like she was crazy but fortunately didn't hesitate to get moving. It wasn't until they were off the resort property and a few miles away that she finally felt like she could breathe. Sagging against the back seat, she immediately began searching for flights back to North Carolina. It didn't take long for her to realize she might not be leaving California or even the Lake Tahoe area tonight. Muttering a curse, she continued to search.

"Are you okay?"

She wanted to roll her eyes at that one. Did she *look* like she was okay? She was sitting in the back of a Toyota Corolla in a wedding gown and heading to the airport alone. However, she didn't think the poor guy would appreciate her sarcasm and opted to bite her tongue.

"Um...yeah," she said with a small smile. "Just...I'm not having any luck finding a flight out tonight." She scrolled the screen some more. "Where's the next closest airport?"

"That would be Sacramento. But it's two hours away in the opposite direction," he explained. He looked like he was close to her age, maybe a few years younger, and Grace remembered the app saying his name was Mark.

"Thanks, Mark. If I happen to find a flight out of Sacramento, would you be willing to drive me there?"

"Uh...I'd have to adjust the route and it's not that easy to do," he said with some hesitation. "I mean, we'd have to pull over somewhere so I could do it and..."

He prattled on a bit about all the steps it would take for him to change the route, but Grace wasn't fully paying attention. Her main priority was finding the first flight she could to get out of here. Unfortunately, it didn't take long for her to realize it wasn't going to happen. She was stuck. Her only hope was to book a flight for first thing in the morning and find a hotel as close to the airport as possible.

And pray it was next to a mall so she could buy a change of clothes.

Her phone began to ring, and Grace was surprised it had taken this long for it to start. Jared's name and picture came up and she felt sick at the sight of him. She immediately rejected the call and did a quick swipe of her screen to block his number. Not that it would stop him. All he'd have to do was grab someone else's phone and try again. Still, it was a start. Next, she turned on the do not disturb feature on her phone so she wouldn't be bothered for a little while.

"Do I need to turn around?" he asked, interrupting her thoughts.

With a weary sigh, she put the phone down. "No. We can keep going. There are no available flights tonight. I'll have to find one for the morning."

"I don't know where you're trying to go, but you could always rent a car and drive."

Again, she suppressed the urge to roll her eyes but...the idea had merit. Sure, a cross-country drive wasn't ideal, but it would give her plenty of time to clear her head. There would be no distractions and no chance of Jared–or anyone else for that matter–coming to talk her out of what she was doing.

"Mark," she said excitedly, leaning forward, "you're a genius!"

He smiled at her in the rearview mirror. "Wow. Thanks!"

"Okay, so where is the closest rental car place? I mean,

we don't have to go all the way to the airport for that, do we?"

"It might be easier, and considering it's a Saturday night, I would imagine the smaller places might be closed already. The airport car rental offices have to stay open later." He shrugged. "At least, I think they do."

Maybe he had a point, but reaching for her phone, Grace figured she could find that out for herself without any problem. "Aha! There is a car rental place just outside of Carson City and it doesn't close until eight!" She leaned forward in her seat again. "Can you get me there by eight, Mark?"

It had just started to rain, so he flipped on the windshield wipers and grinned at her. "As long as this rain stays light, we shouldn't have a problem."

Relaxing back in the seat, she felt like things might finally start going her way.

"Dude, are you all right?"

Finn Kavanagh was so busy muttering curses that he almost didn't hear the guy. Pacing back and forth in the crowded parking lot, he wasn't expecting anyone to come up and talk to him. "Yeah. Peachy, except my car is gone."

The guy looked at him in shock. He was glassy-eyed and looked no older than twenty; there was no doubt he'd used a fake ID to get into the casino, and right now was of completely no use to Finn.

"You gonna call the cops?"

Under normal circumstances he would have, but considering he knew *exactly* who had taken his car and why, it was pointless.

But he wanted to. Boy, oh boy, did he want to. Cursing again, he paced and turned and...oh, right. He still had an audience. "Uh, no. No, I'm just gonna call...a cab or something." With a forced smile, Finn walked back toward the casino as he pulled out his phone. With the help of an app, he knew he could have a ride here in less than five minutes, but he had a call to make first.

Pulling up the number, he hit send and–surprise, surprise–it went right to voicemail.

"Hey, Dave," he said through clenched teeth. "Classy move taking the car. Where the hell are you? In case you've forgotten, I'm eight hundred miles from home, and I got here in the car you currently hijacked, you son of a bitch! You need to get back here and..."

Beep!

If he didn't need the phone so damn much right now, he would have tossed it in frustration. Not that he expected his brother to answer the phone, but he also didn't expect the bastard to leave him stranded in Carson City over a petty fight.

Okay, so *maybe* pointing out how irresponsible his brother was wasn't the smartest thing to do, but who knew he'd be so willing to prove Finn right immediately?

They had decided to take this road trip together as a way of bonding. Honestly, they had never gotten along, and after trying again and again, to find Dave jobs and keep him from mooching off their parents, Finn thought the time away together would help. The idea of them being in neutral territory and away from prying eyes seemed perfect.

Clearly, he was wrong.

Now he was stranded. Dave had his car and Finn needed to get home to Atlanta so he could get back to work. Granted, he was his own boss, but the garage could only run for so long without him. Actually, it probably would be fine without him for a while, but he was responsible and the garage was his baby. He hated being away from it any longer than he had to be.

And that just filled him with rage again because thanks to his brother, he had no choice but to delay his return. Chasing Dave across the country wasn't going to be a quick and easy task, no matter how much he wished it could be.

Looking at his phone, he did a quick search for car rental places in the area. There weren't many, and the smarter thing to do would be to just go to the Tahoe airport, but that was wasting time he didn't have. The sooner he got on the road, the better chance he had of catching up with his wayward brother. Once he made a mental note of the closest place, Finn pulled up the app for Uber and ordered a car to take him there. There was no way he was flying home, even if it was the fastest way to get there. Finn had a fear of flying and just the thought of getting near an airplane was enough to make him feel a little sick. Hell, even walking back to Atlanta was more appealing to him than flying.

It started to rain and he groaned. It was the icing on the cake of the crappiest day ever. He'd already lost all the money he'd brought to gamble with and now he was going to have to pay to rent a car to get home. His luggage was in his car because he and Dave had planned on leaving tonight after dinner. As soon as they had finished eating, his brother excused himself to use the men's room and never returned.

Just thinking about it pissed Finn off more than he thought possible.

His ride pulled up just as the rain really started to come down, and he'd never been more thankful for anything in his life. Climbing into the car, he thanked the driver and immediately tried calling his brother again.

"Come on, man," he all but growled into the phone as the call went to voicemail again. "This is bullshit, Dave. It's my damn car and I can have the cops on your ass for this!" His driver eyed him suspiciously, but Finn didn't care. "Just...call me back." Again, the urge to throw his phone was great, but it would hinder more than help him.

Throwing his head back against the seat cushion, he started thinking his plan through. Maybe he should have just stayed at the casino and waited Dave out. His brother was many things, but he wasn't despicable enough that he'd strand Finn and steal his car.

Or was he?

The phone rang, and he nearly jumped out of his skin. "Dammit, Dave, where are you?"

A low chuckle was the first response. "Just drove through Fallon, but I'm considering heading south and going back to Vegas," Dave said. "Remember how cool the strip was?"

Finn mentally counted to ten before speaking. "Fallon's what...an hour from Carson City? How the hell fast are you driving?"

Laughter was the only response.

"Can you please just stay put and I'll meet you there so we can head home like we planned, okay?"

"No can do, bro. You see, you wanted to lecture me on how irresponsible I am, so you shouldn't be surprised by all of this. I mean, we all know Perfect Finn is never wrong."

If his brother were standing in front of him, Finn would strangle him. There wasn't a doubt in his mind that he'd do it. Dave could test the patience of a saint.

"Shouldn't you be trying to prove me wrong?" he asked

through clenched teeth. "I mean, that is what you normally do! Why do you feel the need to prove me right *now* of all times?"

"Ha-ha!" Dave said, laughing heartily. "I don't really care what I'm proving. All I want to do is piss you off just like you pissed me off. Doesn't feel so good, does it?"

"Dave..."

"Dammit, Finn, where do you get off passing judgment on me?"

"Right now, I think I have every right! You stole my car!"

"Technically, I'm borrowing it."

"No, you're not. You're stealing it. Borrowing it implies I gave you permission, which I did not. And how the hell did you get my keys?"

"When you went to the men's room while we were waiting for our food, I swiped them," Dave said flippantly. "So really, you have no one to blame but yourself for leaving them lying around like that."

Pinching the bridge of his nose, Finn had to wonder how he was going to get through this–or better yet, how he was going to keep himself from beating the crap out of his brother when they were both back in Atlanta.

"Dave," he began, trying to be reasonable, "you know I need to get home. Let's just agree that things got out of hand and move on, okay? Now, where are you? I'm in an Uber and can meet up with you."

The low laugh Dave gave as a response did not fill Finn with hope.

Letting out a long breath, he willed himself–again–to stay in control. "It's getting late and we're wasting time here."

"You got that right."

"It's already an almost forty-hour drive back to Atlanta, Dave. Four grueling days of driving," he added. "We weren't going to get too far tonight, but we can make up time if you just tell me where you are so I can meet you."

"Vegas."

"You're not in Vegas!" Finn yelled. "It is physically impossible for you to be in Vegas already! Now enough is enough! Do not make me call the cops! I'm serious!"

"Sorry...bad...breaking...up...later..."

"Don't hang up! Don't hang up!"

Dave hung up.

The things that flew out of Finn's mouth would make most people blush, but he didn't care. When he kicked the seat in front of him, the driver yelled, "Hey!" and that instantly snapped him out of his tantrum. He was screwed; there were no two ways about it. His brother had his car and he wasn't getting it back any time soon. The sooner he resigned himself to that fact, the better off he'd be.

So, he had to rent a car, so what? And so what if he was going to have to stop and buy himself clothes and supplies to get him through the trip? Worse things could happen. But the worst of it all was how it was going to take him longer than the planned four days. Finn believed in being smart and not overdoing things and knew driving for ten hours a day alone wouldn't be smart or safe.

Something Dave had mocked him about on their original trip.

There was a flash of lightning, and the rain was really coming down. At this point, Finn knew he would be smart to grab a car and then find a hotel and start driving first thing in the morning. With a sigh, he sat back and stared out the window until they pulled into the rental car parking lot.

"Holy crap! Did you see that?"

Finn looked out the front window toward the building and saw...wait...what was he seeing? "What the hell is that?"

The driver laughed awkwardly. "Looks like a bride–or at least, someone in a wedding gown."

And sure enough, that *was* what they were seeing. Whoever they were, they fell getting out of the car and were now in a heap of white satin on the pavement. Finn quickly climbed from the car–thanked his driver–and immediately ran over to help her.

At her side, he held out a hand to her and noticed the guy who was with her coming around to do the same. "Hey, are you okay?" Finn asked, noting the dirty gown and the curses flying out of the woman's mouth. He pulled her to her feet and held on until she was steady. The rain was pouring down on them and he did his best to guide them up onto the sidewalk and through the doors of the rental office.

She was a little breathless and pointed toward the car she'd just vacated. "My bag," she said, shaking her hand. "My bag is still in the back seat!"

"No problem," he said, hoping to calm her. "I'm sure your husband will bring it in."

Pushing him aside, she walked back out the door and slapped a hand on the trunk of the car as it was about to pull away. Finn watched with mild curiosity as she opened the back door and grabbed her bag before slamming the door shut again.

Okay, not her husband, he thought.

Because he had manners, he moved to open the door for her. "Thanks," she muttered, shaking the rain off herself– and onto him. He wanted to be mad, he seriously did, but what would be the point?

With a shrug, he walked over to the agent at the counter

and did his best to smile. "Hey...Carl," he began, reading the agent's name tag. "I would like to rent a car."

The agent smiled but it didn't quite meet his eyes. "Then you've come to the right place!" he said in a semi-flat tone. Finn would bet good money this was a repeated exchange at a car rental office.

Beside him, the bride stepped up and said the same thing to her agent–an older woman named Tammy. He looked over and gave her a small smile and wasn't surprised when she didn't give him one back. Any bride trying to rent a car while still in her wedding gown couldn't possibly be having a good day.

Finn handed over his license and credit card and waited. The only sound in the place was the typing coming from Carl and Tammy's computers. Finn looked around and saw the office was a little run-down and there weren't any cars in the parking lot.

That's when he started to worry.

The cars could be around the back, couldn't they?

"Um..."

"Oh, uh..."

Both agents spoke at the same time as they glanced nervously at each other. "Is there a problem?" he and the angry bride asked at the same time.

"Well, it looks like," Carl began.

"There seems to be," Tammy started.

"Oh, for the love of it!" angry bride snapped. "What's the problem?"

Finn had to hand it to her, she was pretty fierce. Even he stiffened up at her tone. Deciding that one of them should be respectful, he looked at the agents and smiled. "Is there a problem?" he asked.

"We only have one vehicle available," Carl said.

"Oh, well...okay." This didn't seem to be a problem for him since he got here first. "I'll take it."

"Wait, wait, wait," angry bride said, moving closer to him. "Why do you get it? We got here at the same time."

"Actually...we didn't," he corrected. "I got to the counter first, and that was after I held the door for you to come back in."

If looks could kill, he'd be a dead man for sure.

"Look, um...I know this is a bad situation," he reasoned, "but it can't be helped. It's been a really bad day and I need this car."

"Oh, really?" she asked sarcastically, motioning to her ruined gown. "And do I look like someone whose day has gone well?"

"Uh..."

"Because it hasn't!" she cried. "If we're going to get into some sort of contest over whose day was worse, believe me, buddy, I'd win!"

He was beginning to see that.

Unfortunately, he needed this car too. Maybe if he reasoned with her...

Holding out his hand, he said, "I'm Finn. Finn Kavanagh. And you are...?"

Swiping her dripping blonde hair away from her face, she eyed him cautiously. "Grace. Grace Mackie."

She didn't shake his hand.

"Look, Grace, it seems like we're both in a bad way right now. But you have to believe me when I say I *have* to have this car. You see, my brother stole my car, and I've got to get back to Atlanta and..."

"Today was supposed to be my wedding day and I found out my fiancé has been cheating on me with his assistant..."

"Okay, that does sound bad, but you see, I've got a business and..."

"And she's pregnant with his baby," she continued. "Oh, and he was planning on divorcing me in six months, so he and his baby mama could be together. He was just using me to get a promotion."

Finn's shoulders sagged even as he bowed his head.

Yeah. She had him beat.

Without a word, he motioned toward the desk and simply gave up. There had to be other rental places in town, right? And if not, he'd call for another Uber and do...something. There was a row of chairs against the wall and he walked over and sat down. He found this place by searching on his phone, so he'd just have to do it again and hope he'd find another one.

Scrolling...scrolling...scrolling...

The rustling of wet satin had him looking up. Grace was two feet away and still staring at him hostilely. "Problem?" he asked, letting his own annoyance come through.

"Listen, it seems to me we've both had a crappy day and...well...I'm heading across country too. So, if you want to share the car..."

He was instantly on his feet. "Seriously?" Then he got suspicious. "Why? Why would you even offer? You know nothing about me, and for that matter, I know nothing about you."

She rolled her eyes. "Both Carl and Tammy mentioned there not being another rental place nearby. The closest one is about twenty miles from here and is closed for the day. Your only other option is the airport and..."

"I'm not flying!" he snapped and immediately regretted his reaction. "I mean...I don't really like flying so..."

"No, I mean there are car rental places there you can

try, but it's still a bit of a drive to get there too." She paused and fidgeted, and Finn figured her dress had to be a bit of a pain to move around in–even more so now that it was wet. "Nothing today has gone as planned and I'm not looking forward to driving across the country alone."

"I get that, but still...how do you know you can trust me?"

"Honestly? I don't. But Carl and Tammy have your license and would know I was leaving with you, so if anything happened to me, you'd be the guy everyone would go after." Then she paused, and her gaze narrowed. "Is there a reason I shouldn't trust you?"

"What? I mean, no! There's no reason," he stammered.

"Tell me about yourself," she said before turning to the curious agents. "You guys listen in on this too. You're witnesses."

"Witnesses? That's just..."

"I'm just trying to be practical, Quinn," she said.

"It's Finn," he corrected and then cleared his throat. "I'm Finn Kavanagh and I'm from Atlanta, Georgia. I was born and raised in East Islip, New York, and moved to Atlanta when I was eighteen. I'm thirty years old and I own my own auto repair shop, Kavanagh's. You can look it up online. We have a website and a Facebook page," he added.

"Tammy, can you check on that please?" Grace called over her shoulder, not breaking eye contact with Finn.

Finn glanced toward the counter and saw both agents typing and nodding, and when Grace looked over at them, they both gave her a thumbs up.

It was ridiculous for him to sag with relief, but he almost did.

"Anything else?" she asked. "What about your family? You married?"

"No."

"Girlfriend?"

"No."

"Boyfriend?"

"No!" he shouted a little too defensively.

"Any siblings other than the car-stealing brother?"

He shook his head. "Nope. Just Dave."

"Why'd he steal your car?"

"It's a long story..."

And for the first time since he'd met her, Grace gave a small smile. "Good thing we've got a long drive ahead of us and you can tell me all about it."

This is crazy, he thought. There was no way he was going to drive cross-country with a complete stranger. He didn't do things like this! He was fairly practical and cautious, and this had disaster written all over it.

Grace walked back over to the counter and Finn followed. "My turn," he said.

"For what?"

"Tell me about yourself."

She leaned against the counter and looked at him with mild annoyance. "Why? It seems to me I'm the one at greater risk here."

He gave her a bland look, crossed his arms over his chest, and waited.

With a sigh, she said, "Fine. Grace Mackie, career coach, age twenty-eight. Recently ran out on my wedding. I was engaged to the cheating jackass for six months and we dated for a year before that. I have two brothers and one sister, who are all happily married to non-cheating jackasses."

"A career coach?"

She nodded. "I too have a website and Facebook page,"

she turned to Tammy. "Executive Career Services by Grace out of Raleigh, North Carolina. You can Google it." They waited all of two minutes before Carl and Tammy gave another thumbs up.

"Looks like we're both who we say we are," Grace said, her smile growing a little.

"Looks that way," he agreed. "The only problem is you're going to North Carolina and I'm going to Atlanta. How's that going to work?"

She considered him for a moment. "I'd be more than willing to go to Atlanta with you and fly home from there. Unlike you, I'm not in a rush. The longer this trip takes, the better."

Finn didn't take that as a particularly good sign, but he wasn't going to question it right now. Hell, if she wanted to camp out in Atlanta once they got there, who was he to argue?

Still, he wasn't so sure this was going to work.

"Are you willing to split the driving?" he asked.

Grace let out a mirthless laugh. "Dude, I was planning on doing *all* the driving a few minutes ago. If there were more than one car here, I *would* be doing all the driving. So the fact that now I don't have to? Um...yeah. I'd say I'd be willing to split it."

Okay, so she was snarky, but he was going to blame it on the fact that she'd had a bad day.

For now.

"We each pay our own way, right? We'll split the cost of gas, but other than that, you're on your own for the things you need."

She rolled her eyes before shaking her head. "Do you even hear yourself? We just met, for crying out loud! Why would I expect you to pay for anything for me?" Then she took a menacing step toward him. "Are you always this uptight and ridiculous?"

"Ridiculous?" he cried, mildly annoyed. "How am I being ridiculous?"

"Um...excuse me," Tammy called out, interrupting them. "But we're getting ready to close so...are you going to take the vehicle? We can put both names on the rental agreement if you'd like, or we can leave it in Miss Mackie's name."

For a moment, neither spoke. Then Grace seemed to relax a bit. She studied him for a long moment before speaking. "So what do you say, Finn Kavanagh? Are we taking this road trip together?" She held out her hand to him, and for a moment, Finn questioned his own sanity for even considering this. Unfortunately, she was his only hope right now.

And before he could question himself any further, Finn met her hand and shook it. "Looks like it, Grace Mackie."

2

THE CAR WAS ACTUALLY AN OLDER Ford pickup truck.

Grace took one look at it and then at her gown and knew somehow, somewhere, the universe was mocking her. Beside her, Finn nodded and said, "It looks like I'm driving the first leg."

She wanted to punch him.

"As long as the first leg takes us to the nearest Target or Walmart," she murmured, "because there is no way we're getting far with this gown in the truck with us."

Clearly, he was a smart man because he opted not to comment. Silently, they climbed in, and Grace searched on her phone for the nearest mall.

"Why couldn't they have some sort of oversized SUV available, huh?" she murmured. "Or one of those old Cadillacs that were like boats? Or a convertible?"

"A convertible would be completely pointless in this rain, don't you think?" Finn asked, and Grace reminded herself that this guy was going to be of zero interest on this trip. It was obvious he was uptight and overly practical, and there wasn't a doubt in her mind he was going to make her crazy sooner rather than later.

Ignoring his observation, she continued to search for the closest mall. "Okay, there is a Walmart about five miles from here," she said, looking over at Finn. He was a fairly tall guy–easily six feet–and he looked right at home behind the wheel of this crappy truck. Being that he was a mechanic, she figured he was figuring out all the things wrong with it. "Will that work for you?"

He shrugged. "Sure. I'm just getting the necessities, not starting a new life."

That was one way to look at it, she supposed. Studying him a little more, she could tell he was tense. Granted, this situation in and of itself was stressful, add that to his brother taking his car and his belongings, and she figured he had every right to be that way. It was a shame too because other than the negative things she was just thinking, he did seem like he had the potential to be a nice guy–decent and somewhat trustworthy. But then again, what did she know? She thought Jared was a nice guy and look where that got her.

And on top of that, he wasn't half-bad to look at–dark brown hair, even darker brown eyes, a strong jaw...he didn't look to be all that muscular, but he was lean and wiry and seemed to be in really good shape.

"Where's your stuff at?" he asked, breaking into her train of thought.

"Back at the hotel where my wedding was supposed to be," she replied, forcing her attention straight ahead. "Once I overheard Jared and Steph talking, I just...I left. I didn't even think of going to the room because I didn't want to draw attention to myself. I just wanted to get out of there before anyone could try to talk me out of leaving."

He glanced over at her for a second. "Do you...I mean...

would you like to go back and get your stuff? We're already leaving at an awkward time and we're not going to get far tonight anyway. I'm sure it wouldn't be a big deal to go back and get your things."

It was a nice offer–especially since she knew how anxious he was to get on the road–but she'd prefer to do as Finn said and grab the necessities rather than go back and deal with Jared. "Thanks, but...I'd rather not. It's late, and the more distance we can put between here and the East Coast, the better."

But it did bring a thought to mind–her stuff. Knowing she should do something about it, she called the one person she tried to avoid like the plague. Scrolling through her contacts, she pulled it up and hit send.

"Hey, Tilly, this is Grace Mackie."

"Oh, my goodness, Gracie! Where are you? Everyone is worried sick! Are you okay? Are you hurt? Sick? Did someone abduct you? Are you safe? Is there something I can get for you?"

Oh, good Lord...

"Um, yeah, Tilly, I'm fine. I'm not at the resort, and um...no one abducted me." Beside her, she heard Finn chuckle. "I ah...I left."

"You left?"

"Yeah."

"But...why? Did you not like your dressing room? Was it too warm in there? Too cold?"

Seriously? Those were the only reasons the woman could come up with for why Grace would walk out on her wedding? Unable to help herself, she laughed softly. "No, Tilly. The room was fine. It was everything else that wasn't."

Silence.

"I was hoping you could still help me with something."

"Of course, Gracie, anything."

It would be wrong to correct her on the name thing, so Grace decided to simply let it go. "I left all of my clothes, my luggage, my...everything, up in my room. Could you please make sure it all gets shipped to me?"

"But wouldn't Mr....?"

"I don't think he's going to be too concerned with my belongings right now," she quickly interrupted. "It would mean a great deal to me if you could handle it. You can ship it all back to North Carolina for me and bill me for the shipping, okay?"

"Absolutely, Gracie. No worries. You can count on me!"

Good to know she could count on someone.

Grace rattled off her address and thanked Tilly at least a dozen times, and when she finally hung up, she was relieved to see they were pulling into a parking spot at Walmart.

"Okay, great!" she said, twisting carefully in her seat. "This is what I'm going to need you to get for me."

"Wait, wait, wait," Finn interrupted and turned to face her. "Why do I have to shop for you? I've got my own shopping to do. And we agreed–just minutes ago, mind you–that we were responsible for ourselves. I'm not shopping for you, Grace."

Her shoulders sagged. "Oh, come on! Seriously? Look at me, Finn! Haven't I been humiliated enough today? Now you expect me to go inside and shop looking like this?"

"Trust me, Grace, no one is going to judge you in there. If anything, I'm pretty sure you won't even be in the top ten most weirdly dressed people in there." He paused and grinned. "I believe there's an entire website dedicated to the crazy way people dress to shop at Walmart. You'll be fine."

She wanted to argue because the thought of facing any more people while wearing her wedding dress was beyond unappealing, but she knew the quickest way to get out of the damn dress was to go inside for herself and shop.

"Fine," she said with a dramatic sigh. "Let's get this over with."

"Thirty minutes," he stated firmly as they climbed from the truck. "Let's give ourselves thirty minutes to get in and done so we can get on the road."

Grace nodded because it all sounded good to her. The sooner they got what they needed and moved on, the happier she'd be.

Once they stepped inside the store and grabbed their own shopping carts, Grace was amazed at how the majority of the people simply glanced at her and kept on walking.

Thank God.

Finn reminded her of the time and walked away. Part of her had hoped they'd shop together because it would make her look a little less pathetic, but...with no other choice, she embraced the spectacle that she was and began shopping.

The basic toiletries were first—shampoo, conditioner, soap, deodorant, toothbrush, toothpaste, and a razor. Her makeup was in her satchel, so she was good there. Thinking quickly, she grabbed a brush and a couple of bands for her hair. Next, she walked over to the women's department and grabbed a couple of pairs of yoga pants, a couple of pairs of jeans, and a handful of t-shirts. Next came tennis shoes, socks, and underwear. The cart was filling up, but she still had a few more things to grab. Two nightshirts and a robe were thrown in before she walked over to the travel section and found a suitcase and travel pillow.

Standing back, she examined everything she had picked and knew it would have to do. If she forgot anything, she and Finn could stop along the way. Deciding she could go and check out, Grace had gone all of five steps when her stomach started to grumble. In all the wedding preparation hoopla earlier, she hadn't eaten. The plan had been to enjoy a big dinner after the ceremony, and with everything she had to do to get ready, she had skipped lunch.

"Snacks," she muttered. "Better grab some snacks." What followed could best be described as a hungry child left unsupervised in a candy store. The top of her shopping cart was covered in every variety of candy bar topped with several bags of chips, some snack cakes, and a six-pack of soda. Smiling with satisfaction, she said, "That should do it."

She spotted Finn on one of the checkout lines and walked over and moved in behind him. He took one glance at her cart and then at her.

"Is this your passive-aggressive way of saying you're hungry?" he asked, one dark brow arched.

"Right now, I should be cutting my wedding cake," she replied sarcastically. "After enjoying a three-course meal that included chateaubriand, grilled scallops, baby asparagus, and a Caesar salad."

"Oh."

"And...I skipped lunch!" She crossed her arms over her chest and gave him a look that dared him to question her.

He stepped closer and examined the contents of her cart and Grace looked around him toward his.

It was way more organized.

And contained a lot less stuff.

"Are you sure you got everything?" she asked. "It doesn't look like you have enough."

Shrugging, Finn began unloading his purchases onto the belt. Grace watched and counted three pairs of jeans, a package of t-shirts, a package of socks, a package of boxers, some kit that contained all the male-essential toiletries, a brush, and a duffel bag.

Clearly, Finn was an efficient shopper.

He shrugged. "Don't need much. This isn't a vacation; it's just so I don't smell while we're driving."

Um...okay, she thought. Most men she knew would be a little more eloquent in describing this sort of thing but whatever. Jared would have insisted they go to a mall to shop and then...nope. She was not going to go there. For starters, Jared would never do a road trip, and second, she didn't want to even *think* about him right now.

The bastard.

Finn bagged up his stuff and paid while Grace loaded her stuff on the belt. The cashier looked at her and then at Finn and smiled broadly. "Honeymoon off to a rough start?" she asked. "What happened? The airline lose your luggage?"

Grace could feel her cheeks heating and didn't know how to respond because, really, did this cashier need to be on the receiving end of all the sarcasm, anger, and snark that was just dying to be unleashed?

Before she could do or say anything, Finn leaned in and laughed. "They sure did! It's been a wild day, and we're anxious just to have some necessities until the whole mess gets cleared up, aren't we, honey?"

She looked at him like he was crazy, but when she realized what he was doing, she began to laugh along with him. "You know it, sweetie pie!" She turned to the cashier. "We know this is just a little bump in the road, and it will give us something to laugh about and tell our grandkids one day!"

Soon the cashier was laughing with them. "You two are adorable!" Then she started ringing up Grace's things.

"Although, just a bit of marriage advice for you...don't pay for things separately! You are one now! Embrace it!"

Grace looked nervously at Finn, who looked away, and she knew he was snickering. She just knew it! Keeping her smile in place, she said, "This will be our last separate purchase, right, baby?"

Grinning, Finn nodded. "Of course, snookums. Now, why don't we let this lovely lady finish ringing you up so you can get changed and we can get going?"

Just the thought of getting out of the gown was enough to spur Grace into action. After she paid, she pulled a pair of yoga pants, a t-shirt, socks, and sneakers from the bags and walked over to the ladies' room. Finn took the rest of the purchases and told her he'd meet her at the truck, and that was fine with her.

It didn't take long, however, for her to realize that this wasn't going to be a quick-change. It had taken the help of Tilly to get into her gown, and no matter how hard she tried, it was impossible to get out of it alone. She was practically sewn into it. She stepped out of the stall and caught her reflection in the mirror and wanted to cry. There was a time when she'd thought this was her dream gown. The salesgirl at the dress shop had said it was a fairytale fantasy kind of gown and had sold her with her whimsical description. The fitted bodice was adorned with exquisite lace appliques and accented with beads and rhinestones. The sheer off-the-shoulder neckline was exactly what she had wanted, and months of working out at the gym meant she could really show off her arms.

But the floor-length skirt had sealed the deal for her. The oversized skirt was embellished with delicate hand-made flowers. The outer layer was made of tulle, the inter-layer was made of silk net, and the lining was made of satin.

The first time she had tried it on, she felt like a princess. And now look at her. She was muddy, the dress was ruined, her makeup was a smeared mess, and she was standing in a Walmart bathroom. Muttering a curse, Grace grabbed her new clothes and stormed out of the ladies' room and out to the parking lot where she found Finn eating one of her candy bars.

"Hey!" she snapped. "What the hell, Finn? Those are mine!"

With a shrug, he laughed and looked her up and down. "Problem?"

"Yes, there's a problem! Why *wouldn't* there be a problem?" she asked sarcastically. "I can't get out of this stupid gown. I can't reach the damn buttons." Turning her back to him, she motioned to them. "Can you...can you please just help me?"

He popped the last bite of candy into his mouth before reaching out and Grace could feel his knuckles gently caress her skin. Tingles of awareness ran down her spine, and she cursed herself for having any sort of physical response at a time like this.

"These buttons are ridiculously small," he murmured as he leaned in close, and now she could feel his warm breath along her spine too.

"I'm in hell," she muttered.

"Excuse me?"

"What? Oh...uh, nothing. Just commenting on how rotten my luck's been today."

She felt his hands down near her waist and quickly stepped aside. "I think that should do it. Thanks." Glancing toward the massive store, Grace considered her options. The rain had stopped, and she was just so damn tired. "Hey, can you just...you know...turn around?"

Finn looked at her like she was crazy. "You're not going to get changed right here, are you?"

"C'mon, Finn. I don't want to hike back inside!" she whined. "My feet are killing me, this dress is wide open now in the back and...please? Just stand in front of me. I'll open the truck door to shield me on one side and you can shield me on the other. I'll be fast, I swear!"

"Grace, you can't be serious..."

And that was it.

She'd hit her breaking point. Stepping in close, she poked him in the chest. "Do you think that maybe–just maybe–something can go my way tonight? Isn't it bad enough that I'm standing here in a Walmart parking lot on what was supposed to be my wedding night? I'm tired, I'm hungry, and all I want is to take this damn dress off! You ate one of my candy bars, so you owe me! Now, are you going to help me or not? Because I've got to tell you, Finn, I'm not opposed to stripping down right here and just getting it over with!"

By the time she was done, she was breathless and shaking with rage, and Finn must have realized it because he turned around and gave her some room. "Wait," he said. Stepping around her, he reached into the space behind the seats and pulled out all the shopping bags. Loading his hands with all of them, he stepped in front of her and turned his back to her. "Extra blockage."

As crazy as it sounded, it was the nicest thing he could have done for her.

"Thank you," she said softly, and then quickly stripped off her dress and pulled on her new comfy clothes.

They had driven for almost four hours after stopping and grabbing a burger at a fast-food drive-thru for Grace, and now Finn's eyes were starting to cross. "I think we need to stop for the night," he said, and beside him, Grace was yawning.

"Okay."

"Can you look up where the closest hotel is?"

"Nope," she replied and yawned again. "Phone's dead, and I didn't think to buy a charger when we were shopping earlier."

Dammit, neither had he.

"Looks like we'll have to shop again in the morning, but for now, let's just hope we can find a place. This town doesn't look overly populated." They had pulled off the highway and Finn knew it showed that there were hotels off this exit, but...he didn't see much of anything. They drove for another couple of miles when he finally spotted the lighted sign of a chain hotel and said a silent prayer of thanks.

Within minutes, they were checked in and heading to their separate rooms with the promise of meeting up in the lobby at seven to grab something to eat before getting on the road. Grace said she'd drive the first shift and Finn was more than okay with that.

Their rooms were next door to each other, and after saying goodnight, he stepped into his room and sagged against the door. In a million years, he never would have imagined himself in this sort of situation–not only with his brother leaving him stranded but taking a road trip with a complete stranger. And yet...here he was.

Stepping into the room, he looked around and cringed a little. It certainly wasn't a deluxe hotel or even a mid-grade one. There was even a part of him that considered sleeping in the truck, but he knew he was just being overly picky. The place was fine for one night. He'd slept in worse places before, and he'd survive this.

The thought of getting a decent night's sleep spurred him to strip down to his boxers and crawl into bed. His mind was still racing, but he knew if he watched a little TV, he'd be able to fall asleep. He was reaching for the remote when he heard a strange sound. Going completely still, he waited and then...

"Dammit," he murmured. Grace was crying. The walls were fairly thin, and he hated how he was going to have to face her in the morning knowing she had cried herself to sleep.

Not that it came as a surprise. She may have been acting like an angry badass all night, but no one could have gone through something like Grace had and not feel even a little bit of sadness. All night he had been on the verge of asking her about all of it–how she was feeling, what she was going to do when she finally spoke to her fiancé, and what was going to happen when she got home–but she was giving off a pretty hard "back off" vibe, and he was smart enough to take the hint.

When she had rolled her wedding gown up in a ball and went to throw it in the dumpster behind the Walmart, he intervened. She might be angry now, but the gown looked pretty expensive, and he hated to think of her literally throwing it away.

She had growled at him but eventually stuffed the dress behind her seat. All the while wearing a pair of black yoga pants and a t-shirt that said, "Make today your bitch," and he couldn't help but think how accurate it was.

After that, it had been fairly quiet except for her request to go through a drive-thru for some food. He was glad she had not only eaten but had eaten a decent meal. Most women he knew would never opt for fast food, but Grace wasn't picky, and he knew she needed some food in her to keep her strength up. Plus, he had been to enough weddings and heard enough stories about how brides starved themselves leading up to the big day in order to look their best. He had no idea what Grace Mackie normally looked like, but other than the bedraggled angry bride look she had tonight, she seemed to be an attractive woman.

Once she was out of the massive gown and high heels, he noticed she was a little shorter than he thought and a lot curvier. Her blonde hair had been up in some sort of twist style, but by the time she changed clothes, half of it had fallen out. Tomorrow morning was going to be a bit like meeting her for the first time because he had a feeling once she had a good night's sleep and had washed this awful day off, she was going to feel a lot better—and look a lot different.

Finn hoped he'd have a better attitude in the morning too.

Which reminded him...

Getting up, he pulled out his phone, and although the battery was low, he knew he needed to try to talk to Dave one more time. When it went to voicemail, he wasn't surprised, and he wasn't overly angry.

"Hey, it's me again," he said wearily. "Can we please try to talk in the morning? I'm sorry if I overreacted earlier. I want to put this all behind us and get home together, okay? So...call me." Hanging up, Finn knew it was all he could do and simply put the phone down and vowed not to think about the situation again until the morning.

Picking up the remote again, he was about to turn on the TV when the crying got louder, and she may have shrieked a little. Now, he didn't know what kind of crier Grace was, but she didn't seem like a shrieker.

Okay, maybe she did–she was a little scary–but still. The smart thing to do was to go check on her and make sure she was going to be all right.

With no other choice, he climbed from the bed, slid his jeans back on, and grabbed his room key. He felt a little dead on his feet, but once he could see for himself that she was going to be okay, he could go back to bed with a clear conscience.

He knocked on her door and waited. She pulled it open only as far as the chain on the old door would allow. Her face was red and blotchy, her mascara completely running down her cheeks. And for the first time tonight, he noticed how blue her eyes were.

"What?" she asked defensively, and Finn knew she probably wished he would just leave her be, but he couldn't.

"I just wanted to make sure you're okay," he said softly. "I heard you crying and..."

"Oh, my God! You can hear me?" she cried and slammed the door shut. He was about to knock again when she opened it. "Sorry, I just...no need for anyone else to hear me." Stepping aside, she motioned for him to come in.

Finn reluctantly stepped inside and saw the same dismal room as he had and wished it was someplace nicer for her. After everything she'd been through today, she shouldn't have to sleep in a dive hotel. He was sure that the resort she supposed to get married at was posh. At least... judging by her gown and the description of the dinner menu, it was.

"I didn't mean to bother you, Grace," he explained.

She waved him off and sat on the bed. "You're not. I was sitting here wishing I could talk to my mom or my sister, my friends, or...anyone, but my phone is dead, and it's like three in the morning where they are, but they're all probably worried sick by now!" She flopped back on the mattress. "What was I thinking? I mean, how irresponsible of me to take off like that! I should have gone in there and confronted Jared and stood up in front of our tiny group of guests and shamed him in front of all of them!"

There was no place else to sit but on the edge of the bed, so he did. "Grace, you weren't wrong for feeling like you had to get out of there. Do you want to use my phone? Or you can use the phone here in the room. They'll just charge it to you when we check out."

Sitting up, she looked at him with wide eyes. "I can't believe I didn't think of that! It's been so long since I've used a landline phone that it didn't even register that there was one right here!" For the first time since he met her, she was smiling–genuinely smiling. Leaning in, she hugged him and gave him a loud, smacking kiss on the cheek. "Thanks, Finn! I'm so sorry I disturbed you. I know you're exhausted, so really, please, go to bed. I'm going to make my calls, and I'll see you in the morning."

She bounded off the bed and reached for the phone. He knew he was all but forgotten and he didn't mind. If making the calls and talking to the people she loved made her feel better, then he was glad he could help. He wished her a quiet goodnight before leaving the room, and her voice drifted out into the hallway as she got her mother on the phone. With another smile, Finn walked back to his room and locked the door behind him.

This time, the noise he heard through the walls was softer and calmer, and he felt relief for her. Maybe he should have called his parents and told them about what was going on. They would call Dave and talk some sense into him. It would be an easy solution, but the last thing he wanted to do was involve them. That was just one of the reasons he'd asked his brother on this trip–so he'd stop leaning so heavily on their folks. By calling them, Finn was putting them in the middle and in the position where they'd have to bail Dave out again.

"Nope. Not going to go there," he murmured, slipping his jeans back off. Tomorrow was another day and he'd deal with his own mess then.

When he was back in bed, he turned on the television. Five minutes later, he was asleep.

The next morning, Finn was down in the lobby taking advantage of the complimentary continental breakfast and waiting on Grace. It was already almost eight o'clock and he was getting a little annoyed. He had almost knocked on her door on his way down but figured she was a grown woman who was capable of setting the alarm and getting up when she needed to.

Clearly, he was wrong.

Taking a sip of his coffee, he contemplated how much longer he should wait before going up and getting her. It irked him when people couldn't be responsible. It had bothered the hell out of him when he had to do things like this for his brother, and it bothered him even more to have to do it for a stranger. He took the last bite of his bagel before clearing the table. His stuff was already loaded in the truck, and part of him was tempted to leave Grace here just as his brother had left him yesterday. They had agreed on a schedule and she was already breaking it. Storming off toward the elevator, he pushed the button as he got himself more and more worked up. The doors opened and he was about to step in when someone walked right into him.

"Sorry," he muttered, not paying attention. He went to step around them when he heard his name. Looking down, he realized he'd walked right into Grace.

Who did indeed look *very* different this morning.

Her blonde hair was long and wavy. Her skin was flawless and her blue eyes were watching him curiously. "You okay?" she asked.

And damn if he wasn't a little tongue-tied. He could handle the damsel in distress. And he could handle the angry badass. But this sassy woman standing in front of him in the snug yoga pants and clingy t-shirt that read "Okay, but first coffee"? Yeah, he suddenly wasn't sure how he was supposed to act with her.

They both stepped off the elevator and she immediately apologized. "I know I'm late coming down here and I'm sorry, but I went to bed late after making like a thousand phone calls, and when the alarm went off, I just kept hitting snooze. Then I took a shower–and was pleasantly surprised at how great the water pressure was–so I stayed in there longer than I should have." She paused and let out a breath. "Anyway, I can tell by your face that you're annoyed and again, I'm sorry. I promise just to grab a cup of coffee to go and maybe a muffin, and then I'll go check out, okay?"

He nodded as something hit him–her choice of t-shirts seemed to tell the story of who she was. It was both interesting and made him a little fearful of what else he was going to find out about her by reading her...breasts.

Yeah. That could get awkward fast.

"Is the coffee good?" she asked before walking away. "I can deal with mediocre coffee, but I draw the line at awful. So, is it awful? Should I get tea instead? Or maybe some juice, and then we can go through a drive-thru at Starbucks or something?"

"Uh...the coffee was good," he said lamely. With a big smile, she walked away.

So...Grace Mackie–when not in crisis mode–was chatty.

This was *not* good news.

Not that Finn didn't enjoy good conversation, but he had a feeling he and Grace probably didn't look at things the same way or have a lot in common. He was not someone who talked just for the sake of talking, and if this brief speed conversation was a preview of how the rest of their interactions were going to go on this trip, he might consider driving through the nights and sleeping in shifts just to get home sooner.

In the blink of an eye, she was on the move and grabbing her breakfast while talking to the breakfast attendant. He heard her laugh and felt a slight tug of interest. He was glad she was happier today and not crying, but...she had a great laugh–a really great laugh. The only problem was...he could easily see Grace being a distraction–a serious one. If she were someone he happened to meet at a bar or through mutual friends, he would have asked her out on a date and maybe even kissed her by now. With everything going on in her life right now, that was not an option. For starters, she was supposed to get married yesterday. Even if she was hurt and angry over her fiancé's betrayal, she had loved the guy enough to want to marry him. And if she was looking for a way to get even, Finn wasn't so sure he wanted to be that guy. Playing the pawn in a revenge hookup or being a rebound guy was not his thing.

Not now. Not ever.

Grace looked over her shoulder at him as she waited by the front desk to check out and smiled.

Yeah. Distracting.

Chances were she was just a friendly person. Just because he was noticing all kinds of things about her that he found attractive did *not* mean the feeling was mutual. More than likely, she was just being nice to him, and he was going to have to force any thoughts of her and all the things he liked about her out of his mind. They weren't going to help the situation and it was already awkward enough with them being confined in the small cab of a truck for the next four to five days.

Raking a hand through his hair, Finn walked out of the hotel and went to stand by the truck. Maybe if he held on to his annoyance at Grace being late, he could forget about the rest. They were going to have to stop for phone chargers at some point this morning. That was a must. Then they were going to continue on U.S. 95 toward Vegas where they could make their first stop and he could take over driving. If they drove in three- to four-hour shifts, no one would get too worn out.

Then an idea hit him.

What if he found out his brother really *did* stop in Vegas? Then he could simply get his car back and send Grace on her way. It was brilliant! She could go to North Carolina, he could go to Georgia, and they'd never have to see each other again. It was the perfect plan and, honestly, the best solution overall. He was mature enough to know he could make it through this road trip with Grace if he absolutely had to, but he was also realistic. If he was already starting to notice all kinds of great things about her—her smile, her laugh, her...everything—then chances were it was only going to get worse the longer they were together. No, the smart thing to do was to plan on going their separate ways in Vegas.

He was almost excited enough to high-five himself but refrained. No need to look like a lunatic in the middle of a parking lot. Once they got going, he'd try to reach out to Dave and find out where he was. If he knew his brother–and Finn was fairly confident he did–he would have driven straight through to the Strip and stayed at one of the hotels. And, again, knowing Dave, he would have stayed where he won the most money–which was the Park MGM.

With a plan in mind, Finn leaned against the truck and waited for Grace to emerge from the hotel, praying she wasn't standing at the front desk socializing when they should have been on the road already.

"That's good," he murmured, "keep that annoyance going, and maybe you'll survive this without making a fool out of yourself."

He was feeling pretty good about being able to do that.

And he was feeling even better about tracking down his brother and getting his car back.

But once Grace stepped out of the hotel and she spotted him, she waved, and her smile grew. In the light of day, she looked even more attractive, and her snug t-shirt and yoga pants showed off a fantastic figure. When she was beside him, she rested one smooth hand on his forearm and he could smell the strawberry shampoo she must have used.

"Okay, I'm up first, right?" she asked happily. But before he could answer, she was already on the move and walking around to the driver's side. "Let's do this!"

And at that moment, Finn knew he was in deep trouble.

3

Okay, so clearly Finn wasn't a morning person.

And possibly not an afternoon person either.

Honestly, Grace wasn't sure what kind of person he was because he had kept himself fairly busy on his phone once they had stopped and purchased new phone chargers. He had mumbled something about his brother and when she tried to ask about him, Finn turned on the radio.

At a high volume.

Message received.

"When we get to Vegas, let's stop and grab some lunch," he said sometime later.

Snark was her first reaction, but she kept it to herself. "That sounds great," she replied with a big smile. "I've never been to Vegas. Do you think we can stop at one of the hotels?"

Finn turned to her and for the first time today, smiled. "Actually, uh...yeah. Sure." Then he paused as if thinking about something. "How about the Park MGM? We stayed there on the way out here and it was great. They have a really good restaurant there and you can get a burger or a sandwich or even a salad. Will that be okay?"

Grace didn't have a clue about the hotels in Vegas, so she'd take his recommendation. "Absolutely! I'm just excited to see what all the fuss is about finally."

"Fuss?"

She nodded. "So many of my friends have done weekends in Vegas, but it was never something that interested me. I'm not a gambler and I'm not into overpriced shows, so...it seemed pointless."

"There's definitely a lot to see and do even if you're not a gambler," he explained. "I've been there a couple of times. It's something Dave and I do together."

"And Dave is your brother, right?"

Now it was his turn to nod. "Yeah. This trip was supposed to be about us bonding. It was his idea to extend the trip and go to Carson City. He said he'd heard the casino there could rival any Vegas one. I was doubtful, but I was trying to go with the flow and humor him." He shook his head. "And look where that got me."

"Have you heard from him?"

"I've been texting him all morning and haven't gotten a response. Not that I'm surprised." He paused. "Then I checked in with my shop to let them know I was going to be a bit delayed coming home. I know I'm not going to be gone an extra week or anything, but my guys know I'm pretty punctual. If I'm going to be even a day late, I want them to know."

"Your own repair shop, huh? What's that like?" It wasn't like she was particularly interested, but at least he was talking to her. Singing along quietly to the radio was fine, but she preferred talking when someone was driving with her.

"It's like...having a repair shop," he replied and went back to texting.

She sighed.

Loudly.

"Would it kill you to have a conversation with me?" she snapped. "I mean, we have several days of travel ahead of us and it would go much smoother if you weren't sitting there pouting."

He looked at her with wide eyes. "Pouting? I am *not* pouting."

"Oh, please, you are the king of pouting right now," she retorted. "For the love of it, Finn, we get it. You're pissed at your brother and you have every right to be. You're pissed that you're stuck in this truck with me, but hey, too bad. Right now, I'm not too thrilled about being stuck with you either."

"I didn't say that..."

"Then maybe you should tell your face because *that* is clearly saying how annoyed you are with me." And dammit, that bothered her. She'd already been majorly rejected–even though she hadn't realized it was happening–by her own fiancé, the last thing she needed was such blatant rejection from Finn. A stranger.

Ugh...whiny much?

Beside her, Finn fidgeted in his seat before looking at her. "Okay, fine. Maybe I am..."

"Pouting?"

"No," he said with annoyance. "Maybe I'm not being very social. You have to understand–I'm a fairly regimented guy. I like to have things planned out and then have them go according to schedule. And in the last twenty-four hours..."

"Nothing has gone as planned."

"Exactly!" He let out a long breath and turned his head

to look out the window. "It's not you, Grace, and I'm sorry for making you feel bad. But..."

"I get it, okay?" she interrupted. "You had a plan last night to get on the road with Dave and he bailed. Then you got stuck with me and I overslept, so really, I'm the one who's sorry. I promise it won't happen again." She paused and thought about it and knew she needed to be a little more considerate of Finn's feelings. "How about you make the plan for the rest of this trip? Tell me exactly what it is you expect and I promise to make it happen. How's that?"

He looked at her like she was crazy. And maybe she was.

"I bet if you had some sort of spreadsheet, you'd be really happy, huh?" she teased. "Or like, a laminated schedule that we could tape to the dashboard to make sure we were staying on task."

"Now you're mocking me."

She shrugged. "The mood needed to be lightened. So, come on, what's the plan? At least for the rest of the day."

The silence stretched so long that it got awkward, but Grace chalked it up to Finn just thinking things through. She noticed that his brows furrowed and his jaw tensed when he was thinking hard; right now she was pretty sure he might be cracking a molar with how tense his jaw looked.

"Finn?"

"Fine. I wasn't going to share this, but...there's a reason I wanted to stop in Vegas."

"I thought it was probably because it was just the logical choice. The right number of hours for me to drive, places where we could stop and eat..."

"Well, yeah, but...that's not all."

"O-kay..."

"I think Dave is there and I'm pretty sure if he is, he's at the Park MGM."

"What?!" she cried. "So you were...what...just going to casually have us stop there for lunch and then go looking for him without telling me?"

"Uh..."

"Because that is just ridiculous! I mean, I get it. I understand why you want to stop and see if you're right, but why not tell me about it? I'm not the one in a rush to get home! You are! And don't you think having two of us working together to see if your jerk of a brother is really hanging out in the casino would be a hell of a lot faster than you doing it alone?"

"Um..."

"And you know what? I resent the fact that you would keep a secret like that from me!"

"A secret from you? Grace, don't you think you're being just a wee bit dramatic?"

Honestly, she knew she was. But again, it was nice to have him talking and if teasing him and getting him all riled up was the only way she could do it, then so be it. Plus, it felt really good to have a little fun and distract herself from her own shit-show of a life.

"Dramatic? *Now* you think I'm dramatic? You are unbelievable, Finn Kavanagh. Completely unbelievable!"

"*Me?* I'm...how...you know what? You're crazy! And for your information, I only came up with the idea this morning while I was waiting for you to finally get your ass out to the truck, which–by the way–took ridiculously long! And it's not like I'm some scheming mastermind who's been working on some sort of nefarious plan for ages! In case you've forgotten, this all just happened less than twenty-four hours ago!"

She laughed. Like a hearty, can't breathe kind of laugh. Wow. When Finn got going, he really got going. Slapping her hand on the steering wheel, she let herself cackle and enjoy the moment. When she looked over at him, she saw he was smirking too. "Nefarious plan? That's awesome!" she said before cracking up again.

It didn't take long for Finn to start laughing and at that moment, Grace knew she had done the right thing. He had been all uptight and tense, and now he looked way more at ease and relaxed. When they both finally calmed down, she looked over at him and grinned. "There now, don't you feel better?"

He was kind of adorable when he was confused. "Feel better? What are you talking about?"

Rolling her eyes, she reached over and playfully patted him on the arm. "I'm talking about you sitting over there looking so serious and plotting nefarious ways to catch your brother!" She chuckled again. "Like I said, I get why you want to do this, and I am totally with you. I'll help in any way I can." Pausing, she smiled at him. "You're not alone in this. I've totally got your back."

He looked at her like he didn't believe her even for a second. "Seriously?"

"Uh-huh. Trust me, I hate when someone does something dishonest. It's probably one of my biggest pet peeves– and that was before my whole wedding fiasco."

"Can I ask you something?"

"Sure."

"How'd it all go last night? Did you call your fiancé?"

"Ex," she corrected. "*Ex*-fiancé and...yes." God, she really didn't want to talk about this, but considering how big of a deal she just made over his situation, how could she possibly not?

"And? How did it go?"

She groaned and found herself gripping the steering wheel a little harder just thinking about how anticlimactic the call had been. "Well...Jared claimed he was worried sick about me, but once I assured him I was fine and told him the reason I had left, he seemed a whole lot less concerned."

"I swear, Grace, half the time I have no idea what you're talking about. What does that even mean?"

"It *means* he wasn't apologetic for having the affair; he was sorry for getting caught." She glanced over at him and saw the look of disgust on Finn's face as he shook his head. "So yeah, he told me he really appreciated all the work I've done to help him get ahead at work and hoped I'd still consider keeping him on as a client since he feels I would be a great help in getting him the junior vice-president position he's been vying for."

"*What?!*"

Looking at Finn again, she nodded. "Oh, yeah. I've been grooming him for this position for months! His bosses love me–and I mean, *love* me. Their wives and I go out together all the time and they constantly say how I'm the reason Jared's gotten as far as he has in the company."

"Wait...and he thinks you'll continue to help him?" Finn asked incredulously. "Why?"

"According to his way of thinking, I owe him."

"*How*? How could he even think such a thing?"

Grace was thankful she wasn't the only one who saw how crazy her ex's thought process was. "Well, he paid for the wedding–the one that didn't happen–so he's out all that money. And to make it up to him, I should make it look like our breakup was amicable so his bosses will still consider him for the promotion."

"And without you, he doesn't think they will?"

She couldn't help the evil grin she gave him. "I already texted all of them last night while you were driving and told them what he did and who he did it with. But...Jared doesn't know that yet. He won't realize it until he goes back to work in a week." She let out a mirthless laugh. "And he's taking Steph on our honeymoon. He tried to get me to reimburse him, but I politely declined."

"Wow," Finn said with disgust, shaking his head. "Just...wow."

"Yeah. Tell me about it."

"I asked him why he didn't just marry her while the whole wedding was set up. Do you know what he said?"

"I'm almost afraid to ask."

Turning her head toward him, she smiled. It was crazy how the two of them had met, and it was less than twenty-four hours, but...she was really starting to like him. When he wasn't all tense and twitchy, he was a pretty cool guy–one she enjoyed talking to.

"He said things were so chaotic that he didn't even think about it and now he was disappointed they hadn't."

"Wow."

She chuckled again. "I know, right?"

They drove in silence for a few minutes before Finn spoke again. "Can I ask one more thing?"

"Go for it."

"From the very little bit of information I have, this guy sounds like a complete douche. What on earth did you see in him?"

Good question.

All night she had asked herself the same thing. What happened? When did he change? And then...did he change, or did she never realize just how self-centered Jared was? Unfortunately, she didn't know. Her emotions were running too high right now for her to think too deeply or too clearly about it. In time she knew she would, but right now, she couldn't. "I honestly don't know," she replied. "I feel like an idiot for not seeing it sooner–not seeing how this was the kind of person he is–but..."

Finn reached over and placed a hand on her leg and gave it a gentle pat. It was such a small gesture and yet it was the most kindness Grace had felt in a while. So much of her time had been spent focusing on Jared, this stupid wedding, his friends, his job...she had seriously lost herself at some point and didn't have her usual support network of friends and family around her as much as she would have liked.

That was all going to change once she got home–something she promised her mother when they talked last night.

"Hindsight and all," Finn said, interrupting her thoughts. "You were in love, and it can make us blind to the things we don't really want to see."

"Speaking from experience?" she asked and found she was incredibly curious about Finn Kavanagh beyond the whole car-stealing-brother drama.

He shrugged. "Yeah, but it was a long time ago. She was more into having someone support her so she wouldn't have to work. I'm glad I figured it out before I could ask her to marry me." He paused. "It hurt but I was more disappointed than anything else. We had a lot in common and I thought we were in love, but...she wasn't."

"And you were?"

Another shrug. "I think I was at the time, but I got over it fairly quickly so maybe not."

"Wow, that's kind of sad."

"I guess," he said quietly. "Like I said, we had a lot in common and we were good friends, but, ultimately, I think I just got comfortable. There was no...I don't know...*passion* to our relationship.

Then he must have realized what he'd just admitted and began stammering and trying to explain himself.

"I...I mean...we had a good sex life and all. Like we had a *lot* of sex. All the time," he explained nervously. "I just meant there were no real strong feelings toward each other. That's what I meant by passion."

"Relax, Finn," she said, mimicking his move by patting his leg. "I wasn't judging or looking for that kind of information. A little TMI at this stage of our relationship, don't you think? But still, it's kind of sad. How long were the two of you together?"

"Three years."

"Yikes. Almost twice as long as I was with Jared."

"Which brings us back full circle, how did you guys leave it last night?"

With another sigh, she gave him a sad smile. "He truly believes I should help him, I said I wouldn't, he told me he would be marrying Steph, and I wished him well." She shrugged. "And that was it."

"I'm not going to lie to you; I was expecting a lot more drama."

"You and me both."

They grew silent again and for the first time all morning, Grace didn't mind. Up ahead was a sign saying Las Vegas was twenty miles away and she found herself pushing a little harder on the gas pedal. Things didn't go well for her and Jared and she didn't get nearly as much satisfaction as she thought she would get out of confronting him, but now was Finn's chance to do the same to his brother.

And she was going to do everything in her power to help him.

You would have thought he had taken her to Disneyland with the way Grace was practically bouncing on her feet as they made their way down the massive corridor to the casino. Signs and posters were boasting about all of the entertainment the resort had to offer, but Finn had tunnel vision and was only interested in finding his brother.

"Oh, my gosh! Lady Gaga?" she cried. "Is she here? Really? Is there a show? Can we get tickets?" She was looking around frantically as if she thought the singer would be casually walking around with all the guests.

Finn fought the urge to roll his eyes even as he laughed softly beside her. He'd never seen anyone so excited over a casino before. "You know why we're here, right? Dave loves blackjack so we're going to go and scope out the tables to see if we can find him. Then we'll grab some lunch."

"And we couldn't just ask for him at the front desk...why?"

Technically, they could, and for reasons he couldn't explain, Finn was unwilling to go the easy route. He wanted to catch Dave in the act, get his keys and his car, and have it play out very dramatically. Why? Because he felt like Grace needed it.

Okay, he needed it too, but this was primarily for Grace.

"Because I don't want to waste time," he snapped. "Now that we're here, I just want to get this over with."

"Jeez, unclench, Finn. No need to get so snippy."

"I am not...snippy."

She snorted at that statement. "Right. And you don't pout either."

They were on the casino floor and his heart was racing as they made their way around. It was loud and crowded and smoky, but Finn was a man on a mission. Behind him, he heard Grace call out his name and knew he was going to lose her because she was easily distracted by everything she was seeing and couldn't keep up. Reaching back, he snagged her hand in his and pulled her along with him. Maybe she said something to him, maybe she didn't. Either way, he could see the tables he was looking for, and sure enough, he spotted his brother. He stopped so abruptly, Grace plowed right into his back.

"Hey! What the hell, Finn?"

Tugging her around to his side, he pointed straight ahead. "I knew he'd be here."

"Holy crap." She looked up at him. "I have to admit, I thought you were a little crazy to be so confident in this, but clearly I was wrong. You're good. So now what?"

Good question. It would be easy to just storm over to the table and confront his brother, but he knew that wouldn't work. He had to be a little clever if he was going to outsmart him.

And by outsmart, he meant get his keys and leave Dave here to find his own way home.

"Want me to go over and sit down next to him? Maybe flirt a little and distract him before you come over and ambush him?" Grace asked, her eyes wide with excitement.

Placing a hand on her shoulder, he gave her a friendly pat. "While I appreciate the offer, I've got it from here. Why don't you go explore and I'll text you when I'm done?"

"How long do you think you'll be?" she asked as they exchanged numbers.

"I wish I knew, so don't go too far."

With a nod, Grace walked away, and he was too focused on his own moves to even think about what she was going to do. Even if she didn't gamble, he had no doubt that she would be curious and probably walk around a bit. Either that or she'd go in search of Lady Gaga.

With his mind made up, Finn strolled over to the table and took a seat beside his brother and put his money on the table.

Dave grinned and let out a low laugh. "Color me surprised. I thought you'd be halfway back to Georgia by now."

It wasn't the time to point out how that was literally impossible.

Finn shrugged. "You mentioned Vegas and I figured I'd stop on my way through. And, knowing you, I knew I'd find you here playing blackjack."

Looking over at him, Dave winked. "Winning too."

"Good for you, man." He looked at the dealer and at his cards. "Hit me."

"I'm not leaving, Finn. I'm going to hang here for a few more days and then head home so...obviously you've rented a car, so you should just get going. I'll return yours when I get back."

Leave it to his brother to think he was in control even when he was dealing with Finn's belongings. "Personally, I don't care how long you stay here. But I'm taking the car." He examined his cards and looked at the dealer. "Hit me."

"Twenty-one! Congratulations, sir," the dealer said, and Finn smiled with pride.

Dave looked over at him with mild annoyance. "Then how the hell am I supposed to get home?"

"Well, like me, you'll figure it out. If you're winning so much, you can probably fly home, so...just give me the keys, and I'll be out of your way." He was about to place another bet when Dave slapped a hand down on the table and stopped him.

"You think you're gonna just waltz in here and get your way?" he sneered.

"Is there a problem, gentlemen?" the dealer asked.

Finn knew any minute some sort of casino security would be approaching. Looking at his brother, he quietly stated, "You can either give me my keys or I will tell security you stole my car. Considering my name is on the registration and insurance cards, it won't be hard to prove. Your move." And with a smug smile, he waited.

As predicted, two security officers approached. "Let's take this away from the table, please," one of them said, and as Finn stood, Dave glared at him.

"There's no problem, sir," Dave said stiffly.

But that wasn't enough for Finn. "Keys, Dave."

"Obviously, I don't have them on me, Finn. They're up in my room."

"Then I guess that's where we're going." He turned to thank the security officers when Grace came running over.

"Oh, my gosh, Finn! You're never going to believe this! Look!" She was tugging on his arm and he saw a bucket in her other hand. "I won! I won! I was playing the quarter slots and I won five hundred dollars!!" Then she hugged him hard and he didn't have a choice but to hug her back. "I can't believe it! Isn't it exciting?"

Finn noticed his brother staring at him with a smirk, and the two security officers were still standing close by. "Um...Grace?"

She pulled back and looked up at him again. "Yeah?"

"I was just about to get my keys back from Dave, so..."

"Oh! I'm sorry! I totally wasn't thinking!" Turning, she looked at Dave and gave him a hard stare. "You're a real jerk, you know that?"

Dave's eyes went wide. "Uh...what?"

"You heard me! You. Are. A. Jerk. How could you steal your brother's car and leave him stranded like that?"

"You stole this man's car?" security guy number one asked.

"Um…"

"He did!" Grace cried, pointing at Dave. "He totally did and left him stranded in Carson City!"

The security guys looked at Dave and then to Finn. "Is this true?"

Dammit. He really was only bluffing about telling security about the car thing, but now that Grace had put it out there…

"Wait," Dave said, holding up a hand and looking at Grace. "Who the hell are you?"

"I'm Grace Mackie, a friend of Finn's, and I think you're a really crappy guy, Dave, for what you did!" She was at least eight inches shorter than Dave and right now, she reminded Finn of one of those scrappy little dogs who didn't realize how small they were.

Finn reached out and put a hand on her shoulder and gently pulled her back. "Easy there, killer. Can you…can you please give us a minute?"

Grumbling under her breath, she stepped aside, and Finn addressed the security guys first. "This is my brother, and yes, he did take my car and left me stranded in Carson City. I came here to simply get it back from him and go. I wasn't looking for any trouble."

"Do you want to press charges?" security guy number two asked.

It was on the tip of his tongue to say yes, but he knew it would only make him look like the bad guy. "I don't think so," he forced himself to say. "I just want the keys."

"Fine. Whatever," Dave said. "I just need to go get them. I'll meet you back here."

It was funny to see the serious security guys smirk along with him.

"Nice try, Dave. I'm going with you." Then he looked to the officers and said, "Actually, I think we'll *all* be going with you."

They nodded in agreement.

"You're such an ass, Finn," Dave grumbled as he turned and walked away.

They all went to follow when another call for security must have come in because security guy number one said, "Sorry, sir. You'll have to handle this family dispute yourself," before they headed toward the far end of the casino.

By the time Finn turned back to his brother, Dave was gone. "Son of a bitch!"

Grace looked around and shouted, "He went that way!" and took off after him, leaving Finn no choice but to follow.

They wove their way through the crowds with coins falling out of her bucket, but it was nearly impossible to see which way Dave had gone. After several minutes of searching, he reached out to Grace and stopped her. "He's gone."

"No, he's not. Let's go to the front desk, find out what room he's in, and go there! We can reach out to security again to make sure he can't leave," she said firmly. "Now come on!"

She was definitely a little spitfire, and Finn did exactly as she asked. They were both breathless by the time they got to the front desk and he took a minute to compose himself before speaking.

"I'm looking for Dave Kavanagh's room, please."

The attendant smiled at him and said, "I'm sorry, sir. We can't give out that information."

It took every bit of self-control not to dive over the desk at her.

"Can you at least confirm he is a guest here?" Grace chimed in. "We have a bit of a situation here–he stole our car, and we chased him here from Carson City. Security was supposed to escort us to his room, but he took off before they could."

"Oh my," the clerk, typing furiously on her keyboard. She frowned and looked at the two of them. "I'm sorry. There's no Dave Kavanagh staying with us."

"Are you sure?" Finn asked. "It's Kavanagh with a K."

She nodded. "I tried it with both a C and a K, and there's no listing for a Dave or David Kavanagh."

Something in the way she said that made him stop and think. Feeling his entire body tense up again, he asked, "How about Finn Kavanagh? Does he have a room?"

She nodded. "Yes. There is a Finn Kavanagh who checked in this morning."

Whipping out his license, he showed it to her. "I'm Finn Kavanagh, and I'd like a key to my room."

"What?!" both Grace and the clerk cried in unison.

"I can't believe I didn't think to check my credit cards last night after he left! I was so concerned about the car that it was all I could focus on." He skimmed the contents of his wallet, and, sure enough, his American Express card was gone.

"Sir, I can't just give you a key to a room you didn't pay for."

Leaning forward, he studied her name badge and did his best to stay calm. "Julie," he began, "may I speak to your manager? Please?"

"Finn," Grace said, her hand on his arm. "What are you doing?"

"Taking control of the situation. I'm done being played. This has gotten completely out of hand. He thinks he's so damn smart. Well, this time, I *will* press charges."

"Look, I am all for putting your brother in his place, but...this could get really complicated."

"Things are already complicated, Grace!" he snapped. "He stole my car, my credit card, and God knows what else! This ends now!"

"Mr. Kavanagh, I'm Mitchell Roberts, one of the managers here at Park MGM. How can I help you?"

It took close to an hour, and by the time they were done, Finn's voice was hoarse, and all he had to show for it was a room at the Park MGM, a canceled credit card, and no car. His brother had left, but now there was a police report about the entire incident. The management had comped them a room for the night, and as he sat down on the corner of the bed, he looked over to where Grace was standing by the window looking down at the Strip.

Finn had tried to reason with both the manager and Grace that they didn't need a room because they weren't staying. But then she'd looked at him with her big blue eyes and her bucket of coins, and he'd caved.

And even if he hadn't at that point, when Mitchell Roberts offered them discounted tickets to see Lady Gaga, it was the point of no return.

They were staying in Vegas tonight.

They were sharing a room in Vegas tonight.

And when she turned and smiled at him, one thing was certain–he was in big trouble in Vegas tonight.

4

Little black dress? Check.

Painfully cute new stilettos? Check.

The promise of an epic night to forget how crappy her life currently was? Super check!

To say Grace was excited about this unexpected detour was an understatement. She knew Finn wasn't thrilled about it, but she thought tonight would be good for him too. He needed a bit of a distraction after the day's events. If they had left after the lengthy discussion with the hotel manager and filing the police report, he would have obsessed about it for the next several legs of the drive. Of course, there was a very real possibility he was going to do that anyway, but for tonight she was hoping he'd be able to relax a bit and have a good time.

Getting the room had seemed too good to be true. Finn had offered to get one of his own, but she reasoned with him that there were two beds. They were going to run all around town until they were exhausted and were only going to sleep there for one night. Plus, she'd explained how much they'd already been through together in their short acquaintance and how sharing a room wouldn't be any big deal.

Luckily, he believed her. The more she thought about it, however, she wasn't quite so sure.

Checking her reflection one last time, she whispered, "Too late to change your mind now."

Stepping out of the bathroom, Grace found him standing by the window, staring down at the Strip like she had earlier. It was a great view, and it was hard not to stand there and just take it in. He didn't turn around and Grace took a moment to admire the view.

Of Finn, not the Strip.

They had gone shopping earlier for dressier clothes and now he was wearing a pair of black trousers and a slate gray dress shirt. She had been right about his physique. He was lean and wiry, and with the way the shirt hugged him, she could see he was muscular too. Her mouth went a little dry and she had to force herself to look away. Those months of abstinence were really starting to catch up to her right about now.

Clearing her throat, she walked over to the window. "Great view, huh?"

Finn nodded but didn't look at her.

"Okay, I know you're disappointed, and again, if it weren't for me, you'd be on your way home."

"Grace..."

"But I want you to know I did this as much for you as I did for me."

He turned his head and looked down at her; his eyes were so dark and intimidating that they were almost black. "What?"

She let out a small breath. "Look, if we had left earlier, we would have gotten in the truck, and with nothing else to do but watch the road, you would have obsessed over every-thing Dave did."

"I don't see how..."

Holding up a hand to silence him, she went on. "And you have every right to do it, Finn, but I think you need to take a little break from the norm right now. The situation with your brother is still going to be here when we get on the road again tomorrow, but for tonight..." She shrugged. "Tonight, let's pretend you don't have a douchey brother and I don't have a cheating ex, okay? For tonight let's just be Finn and Grace, who are going out for a fabulous dinner and seeing a great show..."

"I'm not really a fan..."

"Uh-uh-uh," she interrupted. "Do *not* ruin this for me. That woman has a voice like an angel and it's going to be amazing so just...shush!"

He chuckled, sliding his hands into his pockets. "Fine. So, we're going out for a fabulous dinner, seeing a great show, and...what else?"

"We're going to end the night by hanging out in the casino for a bit and seeing if I can score another win and then, after a nightcap, we'll come up here and sleep way better than we did last night because this room is amazing."

"That is the truth," he said, grinning. Studying her for a long moment, he reached out and touched her arm. "Thanks."

"For what?"

"Because you're right. I would have been miserable and distracted if we left earlier, and it wouldn't have been safe. And while I'm not so sure this is going to be as exciting as you seem to think it's going to be..."

"Don't ruin it..."

He laughed softly again. "I'm still glad we're doing this, so..." He held out his arm to her. "Shall we?"

Hooking her arm through his, she smiled up at him. "We shall."

They had opted to stay in the hotel for dinner–and for everything tonight–and even though she knew it made sense, there was so much out there on the Strip she wanted to see! Was it a mistake to accept the tickets to the show and do everything in-house?

Alone in the elevator, Finn turned to her. "You okay? You look like you're thinking pretty hard about something."

Why deny it? "I don't know. I think I'm having buyer's remorse."

"What do you mean?"

Turning, she leaned her shoulder against the elevator wall. "There are dozens of hotels and casinos on the Strip! Hundreds of places we could eat!"

"I don't think it's that many..."

"And I went and locked us into this one singular hotel on our one and only night in Vegas!"

Part of her wished he'd say they could stay longer, but she knew he wouldn't. Finn was definitely a man with a schedule and a to-do list that was probably a mile long. There was no way he was going to do something sponta-neous–especially not with the situation with his brother still lingering.

Now she hated Dave even more.

"We can totally go someplace else to eat, Grace. There are a lot of places within walking distance and we have plenty of time before the show."

And she knew that he only agreed to the show because she had made such a big deal out of it. That was the kind of guy Finn Kavanagh was apparently. He'd already sacrificed so much for her sake—and she kind of was the reason he didn't get his keys back from his brother. That had been bothering her all afternoon. If she hadn't come over at that point, he would have left with Dave, gotten his keys and...

He'd be gone by now.

And she'd be alone.

Time for a new plan, she thought.

"If you could do anything you wanted to do tonight—go anywhere you wanted to go, eat anywhere you wanted to eat—what would you do?"

He gave a casual shrug—like he always did—before saying, "I don't know. I've been here a couple of times before and seen most of the hotels and casinos, so...there isn't really anything I feel like I haven't seen or done that I wanted to."

Rolling her eyes, she gave him a slight shove. "Oh my gosh! Could you stop being the most neutral and boring person on the planet?"

"What?" he demanded.

"You!" she cried. "You just constantly go with the flow, don't make a scene, accept all the crap life throws at you! Do you ever just do something spontaneous, Finn? Do you ever just say screw it and do something just because it's fun and not because there is some practical purpose to it?"

His expression grew fierce. "You don't know anything about me, Grace. Don't go making assumptions."

"I'm not! Everything I've witnessed about you and everything you've told me about yourself is what I'm basing this on! You took this road trip with your brother because you were hoping to bond with him—not because it was a fun thing to do! You're only staying here for the night because I bulldozed you into it! And you're willing to go see Lady Gaga in concert because I want to! Admit it!"

He sighed loudly but didn't look the least bit put out–the expression was still fierce, but other than that, nothing changed. "I'll admit it's not my top pick–or even my tenth pick–of shows I'd see, but then again, I'm not really a show kind of guy."

Now she turned and leaned her back against the wall and was about to say more when the elevator doors slid open. Once they were walking across the lobby, she tried again. "So, you're not a show kind of guy. That's fine. Then what kind of guy are you? Do you like steaks or burgers for dinner? Do you prefer to go to a nice restaurant or a bar? Beer or wine? Slots or blackjack? Would you ride the roller coaster at the top of the hotel down the street or is the High Roller observation wheel more your speed? Would you do the zipline over at the Rio?" She let out a low growl when he wasn't reacting at all. Tugging his hand, she made him come to a halt. "Do any of those things appeal to you at all?"

He stepped in close, and for a minute, he looked pretty intimidating. Grace swallowed hard and looked up at him.

"I've done all of those things, and yeah, they're fun, but been there, done that. If you want to do those things, then just say so and we'll do them." And then his neutral, easy-going manner was back. "We're here for you tonight. Not me. So if you want to experience all those things, then we will."

And for some reason, she wanted to make it her life's ambition to watch this man lose control and have fun–to see him loosen up and unclench a bit. Tonight was already supposed to be a distraction for him. But now she was determined to experience as much as she could with him so when he looked back at this time he wouldn't be thinking about all the ways his life had gone wrong; he'd remember how for one night, he'd had the best and most exciting time.

Maybe somewhere in the back of Grace's mind she thought she was doing a good thing, but the reality was that Finn was exhausted and he had really been looking forward to the quiet and somewhat boring original plans they made for the night.

If they had opted to call it quits after Gaga took her final bow, he would have been happy.

And, not that he'd ever admit it, but he really enjoyed the show.

After they'd walked out of the theater, Grace was a woman on a mission. She'd dragged him through the casino and out the door onto the Strip and hadn't stopped since. Now they had ridden the roller coaster, ate multiple desserts because–according to Grace–they were adults and they could, and now she was happily walking toward the High Roller. Part of him realized she had no idea what that really was because it was definitely not a thrill ride. It took thirty minutes to do a full rotation, so...yeah. Speed had nothing to do with this particular ride.

They were heading up the block when she stopped.

"Wait...is this it?"

He chuckled. "You see any other observation wheels around here?"

"No, but...is it broken? It doesn't look like it's moving."

"It is; it just goes really slow. Like super slow. Painfully slow," he added for emphasis. Looking at her face, Finn could see her pout. She was clearly disappointed, but he knew once she got over the speed factor, she was going to love the view once they were on it. Taking her hand in his, he said, "Come on."

Grace grumbled the entire time they walked the line, purchased tickets, and even purchased drinks.

He thought she'd at least crack a smile at that one.

There wasn't anyone in front of them and they ended up with an observation pod all to themselves. When they stepped in and the doors closed behind them, Finn stood back and watched Grace take it all in.

"Holy crap," she said in awe. "How many people can fit in this thing?"

"I don't know, maybe thirty? I think that's what I heard someone say once." He was standing in the middle of the pod and watched as she walked around the entire perimeter. "It only goes one foot per second and it takes a few minutes before you start to get a really amazing view of the city. And–to me–this is the best time to do this."

"How come?"

"Because everything's all lit up now."

With a nod, she continued to walk around and take in the sights.

There was music playing, and all of the screens up near the ceiling had something showing on them. Finn knew the recorded message telling them about the wheel would give her all the information she wanted. The view from the top was going to be spectacular. Finn knew this from experience. And he had to wonder what she was thinking as the wheel continued its slow ascent.

"This is amazing." She was practically pressed up against the glass and looking over her shoulder at him. "I didn't think there'd be so much to see because it's dark out, but you're right. This was the perfect time for this." She paused and looked back at the Strip. "And to think, I almost suggested coming here earlier. What would I have done if I missed all this?"

"Well, now you don't have to worry," he said casually. But even as he said the words, he knew if that had happened and they'd come here while it was still light out, he would have consoled her and maybe even ridden the wheel multiple times just so she could get the perfect view. Something about her made him want to make that happen for her—like if he could, he'd darken the sky and turn on all the neon in the city just for her.

What the hell is happening to me?

Her hips were swaying seductively, and she was singing along with Taylor Swift's *Delicate* as they began to rise above the Vegas skyline. She had a decent voice and just like everything else he was beginning to learn about her, Grace Mackie gave one hundred percent to everything she did—whether it was anger toward her cheating ex, celebrating her win on the slots, or totally captivating him.

Before he knew it, Finn was stepping in close behind her—so close they were touching. In an entire pod with over two hundred square feet, the only place he wanted to stand was right here so he could feel her.

And she was warm and smelled so good and...

Grace slowly turned around so they were pressed together from head to toe. Maybe it was intentional, maybe it wasn't, but the slow slide of her body against his was a definite turn on. Finn swallowed hard because he knew what he wanted to do—wanted it possibly more than he'd ever wanted anything in his entire life. But he couldn't do it. He'd already had this conversation with himself. Being the rebound guy or the revenge fling was totally not something he wanted to be.

Her hand skimmed up the front of his shirt before raking up into his hair. "Finn," she whispered, licking her lips and looking at him in a way most men only dreamed of.

Unable to help himself, Finn reached out and gripped her hips. "What are we doing, Grace?"

Her smile turned a combination of impish and sexy. "You're going to kiss me," she said, her voice a little breathless. "And I'm going to kiss you."

He was lowering his head even though he knew this was a mistake. It was crazy and wrong, and he knew better. Then Grace let out a sexy little hum and he was lost. Closing the distance between them, his lips captured hers in a kiss that wasn't tentative–or untamed.

It was perfect.

Holy shit, was it perfect.

Her arms came up to wrap around his shoulders and her breasts pressed seductively against his chest. Her lips were soft and wet and when her tongue came out and touched his, Finn wrapped both his arms around her and completely sank into the kiss. It didn't matter how wrong or crazy it was; there was no one here right now but the two of them and he vowed to himself this one rotation on the observation wheel would be the one and only place this could happen. It would be like they had taken a brief step away from reality for these thirty minutes, and he was going to enjoy every minute of it.

The sounds Grace was making had him harder than he thought possible. He tore his mouth from hers and kissed a path along her jaw and then down to gently bite her throat. "We shouldn't be doing this," he said between kisses. He wanted to taste and touch every inch of her that he could reach.

And he wanted to do it all at once.

"Yes, we should," she countered, nipping at his jaw. "We totally should."

Her nails scratched along his scalp. Her breath was hot

against his skin. And when she lifted one leg to wrap around his waist, he was pretty sure he was being rewarded for being so damn good and responsible all the time.

This was going to happen.

He'd earned it.

His hands skimmed down to the hem of her little black dress–that only hit mid-thigh–and began the slow journey up. Her skin was so smooth, and he'd be lying if he said he hadn't been wondering about what she was wearing underneath it ever since she stepped out of the bathroom earlier.

He was inches away from finding out.

"Finn?" she panted.

"Hmm?" One finger touched lace and he did his best to hold on to some sense of control.

"Are we...I mean...can we...?" she rambled, but by now his hand was covering the lace he discovered–the now *damp* lace–and he liked how she was having trouble organizing her thoughts.

Finesse, he reminded himself. *Have a little finesse.*

But it was pointless. Between the feel of her, the sounds she was making, and the way she was moving against him, any self-control would be useless. Instead, he touched and teased Grace until she was writhing against him. There was a bench seat only three feet away. He could lay her down on it and...

"Oh, God," she moaned, her movements becoming more and more frantic. "Right there. Oh, please, Finn. Don't stop. Please!"

He would give her everything he had and more, he thought. "Come on, Grace," he murmured thickly against her ear. "Come for me."

And she did.

Gloriously so.

Finn gentled his touch as she came down from her orgasm. They were both breathless, and it would take very little effort for him to maneuver them so they could take this to the next level, but...

"Here we go, folks! The last five seconds!" the recording said. They were almost at the top of the observation wheel, and when he looked out over her shoulder, he knew what he had to do.

"Five, four, three..."

Gently, he grasped her shoulders and turned her around to face the view. They were coming up on the top of the wheel where the view was at its best. "Look at that, Grace," he whispered against her ear. "You can see all of Las Vegas from here."

All the lights in the city were on and the timing couldn't have been more perfect for them to stop and see it all.

"Wow," she murmured, her hands planted on the glass. "This is amazing. The view is incredible!"

Finn couldn't agree more, but his view was of Grace with her dress still mildly hiked up and her red thong on display.

It was one damn fine view.

Reaching out, his hands cupped her rear as he leaned in close and pressed against her. The things he wanted to do to her...

"Thank you," she said quietly.

And Finn wasn't quite sure how to respond.

Grace looked at him over her shoulder. "As much as I'm enjoying this view, I kind of wish we were back at the hotel."

It would be at least another fifteen minutes until they were on the ground, followed by another fifteen minutes until they were back in their room.

And that was if they walked really, really fast.

But now that the sex fog was lifting, Finn thought maybe it was better they weren't back at the hotel. If they were, he had no doubt that they'd both be naked by now, and while it would be incredible, his original thoughts and feelings about why this was wrong came back.

Loudly.

Dammit, he hated how loud his conscience could be.

"Grace," he began reluctantly. "I don't think..."

She turned around and placed one finger over his lips to stop his words. "You think too much, Finn. For tonight, can't you just...not?"

Man, he wanted to say yes so badly. He wanted to be the kind of guy who could just throw caution to the wind and have no regrets. Unfortunately, he knew he wouldn't be the only one having regrets come morning. If they continued, how awkward would it be tomorrow when they had to get into the truck together and then keep driving for another three to four days? No. They couldn't do it. It would make an already weird situation worse and he wasn't comfortable going there.

But he also couldn't resist touching her. Reaching up, he caressed her cheek as her hand dropped to her side. "I wish I could, but you and I both know this isn't a good idea. While it might feel really good right now, it would make the rest of the trip home awkward." He saw the disappointment in her eyes and silently cursed himself. "You have no idea how much I wish it could be different–that *I* could be different."

"Can I just ask you one thing?"

"Of course."

"While we're here–alone in this pod–could you maybe just kiss me?" There was a slight tremor in her voice and

Finn knew how much it must have cost her to ask this of him.

He wasn't completely heartless or unaffected.

If anything, it gave him the excuse to live the fantasy for a little bit longer.

"Please," she whispered, and rather than say anything, Finn once again lowered his lips to hers.

They didn't see any more of the view of the Strip.

They kissed as if they had to squeeze in a lifetime of them in the next fifteen minutes.

Which they did.

Finn did his best to memorize everything about Grace– the feel of her skin, how soft her hair was, the way she hummed while she kissed. Someday, after he was back in Atlanta and alone, he would remember this–their brief reprieve from their regular lives. There wasn't a doubt in his mind that it would be burned in his brain forever.

Music continued to blast through the speakers and the lights outside continued to change colors, but Finn didn't pay attention to any of it. His mind was fully focused on the woman in his arms and how knowing her for a mere twenty-four hours had turned his world upside down.

"That's it for our ride, folks," the recording called out, and it was Grace who heard it because she slowly broke their kiss.

"Time's up," she whispered, and those two simple words held far too many meanings.

Reluctantly, he took a step back but took one of her hands in his. As they stepped out of the pod and made their way toward the exit, neither spoke.

As they walked up the crowded side street, they didn't comment on the shops or the people they saw like they had on their way in. Up on Las Vegas Boulevard, they turned toward their hotel and maintained the silence. He had to admit that he liked it better when she was chatty. The walk over had been spent with her barely taking a breath because she was excited by everything she saw and all that she still wanted to see.

Which reminded him...

"You had a list of other places you wanted to see tonight. It's still early." Then he paused and let out a small laugh. "Well, early according to Vegas. We can take an Uber over to the Rio for the zipline, or we can grab something to eat, maybe even sit down for dessert. I don't think all those snacks constitute a proper dessert."

She shrugged, and Finn knew he was going to have to take control to get their night back on track. There was still so much to see and do to call it a night and just go back to the room—and considering how he was the practical one, that was saying something. They had this one night in Vegas and even though nothing was ever going to top what they'd just experienced in the High Roller, he was determined to cross more things off her list.

And he knew exactly where to start.

"Where are we going?" she asked when he began to lead her in the opposite direction of their hotel.

"You'll see," he promised, grinning at her. When they crossed the street and stopped in front of the Bellagio, Finn checked his watch and knew he'd hit this just right. The music started, and he heard Grace's soft gasp. Carefully, he positioned her in front of him and wrapped his arms around her as they watched the fountain show.

He was playing a dangerous game—keeping her close and touching her the way he was, but he couldn't help it. Somewhere in his mind, he reasoned that the Strip was like the observation wheel—it didn't count. It was neutral territory. And as long as they weren't in the hotel room or in the truck, this was all fair game.

The fact that all it was really doing was making him want her more didn't really register with him.

Or he was choosing to ignore it.

When the show ended a few minutes later and the crowd was applauding, they joined in. Finn wasn't prepared for Grace to turn around and launch herself into his arms, kissing him soundly. He placed her back on her feet and rested his forehead against hers. "I take it you enjoyed the show?"

"Oh, my goodness, yes! That was amazing! And I can't even believe I didn't have it on my list tonight!" She stepped back and looked around excitedly. "Where to next? Where should we go?"

Honestly, his first thought was to say to hell with it all and go back to the room, but sanity prevailed. The perfect distraction came to him. "Let's grab an Uber and get you on the zipline!"

"Yeah!"

After that, the night took a completely different turn. The sexual tension was gone and in its place were two friends having an adventure. They rode the zipline, had drinks on the rooftop bar, and got the commemorative photo before leaving. After that, they took another Uber over to the Venetian where they took a gondola ride and listened as their gondolier sang to them. It was a bit cheesy, but Grace seemed to love it.

"I think we need some food, Finn. It's been hours since dinner and all this walking around and sightseeing made me build up an appetite," she said as they stepped outside of the hotel. "And if you can believe it, my feet are killing me, and I'd love to just sit for a while."

It was almost two in the morning, and it had already been a long, mentally exhausting day, but he hated the thought of being the reason she had to call it a night if she wasn't ready to. "So, where would you like to eat?"

"Would you be upset if I said I just wanted to go back to the hotel, grab something from one of the casual places, and relax?"

He couldn't help but laugh. "Upset? I was just thinking how long of a day it's been!"

Looping her arm through his, she rested her head on his shoulder as they walked. "Oh, thank God I wasn't the only one! I feel like a wuss for wanting to call it a night when there's still so much to see and do, but...I'm beat!"

They walked back to the hotel and considered their food options. "What are you thinking?" Finn was hungry, but considering the late hour, he wasn't so sure he wanted to go too crazy and order a lot of food.

"Is it wrong that I want some pizza and a milkshake?"

He chuckled. "Wrong? I wouldn't say that. Although I have to admit, you tend to eat like an unsupervised kid most of the time."

She blushed but laughed with him. "Yeah, well...I feel like I've been starving myself for weeks and I totally deserve this. Normally I don't eat like this, I swear. But I've denied myself a lot of things lately and I'm not going to think about all the calories I'm consuming."

With a curt nod, he stepped forward and ordered a medium pizza.

"Ooh!" she called out. "With pepperoni, please!"

The guy working the counter changed the order and said, "Ten minutes."

Not sure of what else to do, Finn decided it was point-less for the both of them to stand here and wait, and it wasn't going to take both of them to carry it all back to the room either. "Tell you what," Finn said after a minute, "why don't you go up to the room and I'll meet you up there? This way you can take your shoes off and get comfortable. I'll be up in a few minutes."

She smiled with gratitude. "Are you sure? I hate leaving you here by yourself."

He waved her off. "Just go. It's not a problem."

"And you'll get the milkshakes?"

"Shakes? As in plural?" he asked incredulously. "Just how hungry are you?"

Grace swatted at him playfully. "I just figured you were having one too! Oh, my gosh, as much as I deserve pizza at two a.m. I couldn't top that with more than one milkshake!"

"Well, thank God for that," he teased and then gave her a gentle nudge toward the exit. "Go. I'll be up in a few."

With a happy little wave, she was gone, and Finn was thankful to have a few minutes to himself. Earlier, when they had gotten the room, he worried about the sleeping arrangements. There were two queen-sized beds, so he at least had that working in his favor, but that was before everything that happened tonight. How hard was it going to be to stay in his own bed with Grace sleeping just a few feet away?

Now that he knew how she tasted, how she kissed, how incredibly good she felt in his arms, could he really sleep a few feet away from her and pretend it never happened?

You have to.

Yeah. He had to.

While he waited on the pizza, he walked over to get their milkshakes. It wasn't something he would have ordered on his own, but once she mentioned it, it sounded too good not to get one for himself.

She had a way of doing that to him–making him do things he didn't normally do and try things he wouldn't normally try, and for the life of him, Finn didn't know if it was a good thing or a bad thing. All he did know was he was too tired to think too deeply about anything right now.

He gave himself another stern pep talk while he paid for the food.

And all the way up in the elevator.

By the time he stepped out on their floor, he felt mildly in control and knew they could do this. They had their moment of weakness while out on the Strip and now it was over. It was back to reality, and he was fairly certain that now that they were back to normal, Grace would see he was right. Sleeping together wasn't the right thing for either of them. End of story.

Pulling the keycard from his pocket, he opened the door and froze.

Grace was standing in the middle of the room in nothing more than the red lace thong and a matching red bra.

Finn's mouth went dry, and he forced himself to step farther into the room and let the door slam shut behind him. No doubt his jaw was on the floor and he knew his eyes had gone painfully wide.

Along with the rest of him going painfully hard.

"I've been waiting for you," she said softly, seductively.

And all of Finn's plans went right out the window.

5

Never in her life had Grace felt this nervous, but the look of pure desire on Finn's face made it all worth it.

All night she'd thought about this–ever since she stepped out of the bathroom earlier and saw him standing by the window looking down at the Strip–Grace knew this was what she wanted. And it had nothing to do with Jared and getting even or rebounding; this was about her attraction to Finn Kavanagh and wanting this one reckless night with him.

She had promised herself that tomorrow, everything would go back to the way it was, but she wanted this night–*needed* this night. And she needed it with Finn.

He placed the pizza box and their drinks on the dresser before slowly stalking her. She thought the way he moved was incredibly sexy, the way he was pursuing her–like she was going to move or try to get away. Just the thought of that almost had her laughing out loud.

But there was nothing funny about this.

What was going to happen here was very serious. Grace didn't take sex lightly, and she'd never been the kind of woman to have casual relationships or hookups. Back when she first met Jared, it took almost three months before she agreed to sleep with him. That was her usual time limit before taking a relationship to the next level. But there was something about Finn that made her feel like she never had before.

Safe.

Everything about him made her certain he wouldn't be flippant about this either. His earlier refusal to let things go any further proved that. After all, there they were alone in a completely private room on the observation wheel with thirty minutes to kill. He could have taken advantage of her multiple times over and she had no means of escape.

But he didn't.

Instead, he had seen to her pleasure–which she had not been shy about seeking–and took nothing for himself. To be honest, Grace didn't think men like Finn even existed. Like it was some kind of myth–like unicorns or Big Foot–or the sort of thing you only read about in romance novels. In her entire dating life, she'd never met a man like him, and she had a feeling she never would again.

This was a risky move–waiting for him wearing next to nothing. She'd never done anything like this before–never felt the need to. By the time she stepped into the elevator, she knew she'd have to do something drastic to change his mind. She braced herself for the rejection or at least for his explanation as to why this wasn't a good idea. When they were toe to toe, she stiffened her spine and waited.

But his hand reached out and gripped her hair as he claimed her mouth and all she could do was say a silent prayer of thanks.

Yes!

His kiss was wild and frantic and oh so good. This is

what she wanted–to feel Finn lose control. He tugged at her hair to tilt her head back for better access to her, and Grace was completely on board with that. She'd never been kissed like this–like she was vital and necessary for a man's existence. And yet, that's exactly the way Finn was kissing her, and she wasn't sure if she'd be able to settle for anything less ever again.

There was a need for breath–her lungs felt full and she knew all she needed to do was break the kiss for a moment–and yet she couldn't bring herself to do it. Not yet. Just one more taste. One more duel with his tongue. Finn must have felt the same because he abruptly broke the kiss, gulped for air and then dove right back in.

And again, she said a silent prayer of thanks because his lips were back on hers and it was just as glorious and all-consuming as the last kiss. Her hands raked up and down his back before she let herself be bold and simply squeezed his ass.

Damn. It felt even better than she imagined.

And there had been several times tonight when she had imagined it quite vividly.

Then they began to move. A few steps to the left, a few to the right, and a couple back until they landed on one of the beds. She didn't know which one and really didn't care. The only thing that mattered was how he was kicking off his shoes as he climbed up her body. When he stretched out on top of her, Grace almost wept with relief. His body was so lean and warm and wonderful, and it felt amazing to simply wrap herself around him.

Finn lifted his head and looked down at her, his expression fierce, and she feared it was going to happen now–now he was going to give her the lecture and rejection. His eyes scanned her face and she could read his every emotion–the desire, the uncertainty. The silence stretched until she thought she'd go mad. Then, with nothing else to do and too afraid to say anything and risk ruining the moment, she simply held her breath and prayed she was wrong.

"You drive me crazy. You know that, right?" he growled. "This should not be happening."

And yet he wasn't moving away, she realized. Maybe he just needed to say this for his own benefit and as long as he didn't move off of her, she'd gladly listen to whatever dialogue he needed to get out.

"We just met," he said, part wonder, part anger. "There's no way we should feel like this."

It was on the tip of her tongue to counter that comment with all the ways they *were* feeling like this and how it wasn't a bad thing.

But again, she was too afraid to say the wrong thing and then all of this would go away.

Her hands skimmed up his spine, and she wished his shirt was off. She wanted to feel his skin, taste it, scratch it. Just the thought of it had her letting out a soft moan as she arched underneath him.

How was it possible she was ready to have an orgasm just from the feel of his body lying on top of her?

Although really, who was she to complain? Any orgasms she didn't have to give herself were a bonus, weren't they?

Slowly, Finn leaned in close. He kissed her lips, her cheeks, even her eyelids before moving along to nuzzle her neck. She was so certain he was going to keep going when he suddenly lifted his head. "Be sure, Grace."

And that was the thing, she had never been more certain about anything in her entire life. She'd been with other men, loved other men, and almost married another man, and yet none of them made her feel the way Finn did.

It was like she'd been searching for something that was always just out of reach, and his kiss made everything clear. She'd been searching for a feeling–for a connection to some- one–and it pained her how she had been willing to settle for Jared without it. Had she loved Jared? Sure, but not the way a woman marrying a man should. She knew that now.

Wait...how can I even be thinking like this?

"Grace?" Finn whispered, and she knew he wouldn't touch her again, wouldn't kiss her again, until she told him she was sure.

Her hand raked up into his hair as she guided his lips back to hers. "I've never been more sure," she said quietly and then wanted to shout with joy when he kissed her again. It went on and on and on, and it felt even more inti- mate than what they were about to do. Tightening her legs around his waist, Grace pulled him as close to her as they could get with Finn still fully dressed. And as much as she wanted to nudge him along and get him naked, she didn't want this moment to end.

It didn't take long for each of them to grow restless, and this time when Finn lifted his head, he sat up and began to unbutton his shirt.

"Finally," she said with a small laugh. "I was beginning to wonder if you were ever going to take that off." And with each inch of skin he revealed, her hands began to twitch with the need to touch him.

He grinned down at her and he had the sexiest smile, she thought. It was boyish but confident, and everything about him was just so damn appealing. Dark hair, dark eyes, strong, slightly stubbled jaw...God, if ever there was a man to have a wild night with, this was him.

His shirt fluttered to the floor and he placed one hand on her stomach. He was all tanned and rough skin against her own smooth and creamy belly. Even if she didn't know what he did for a living, she'd know by the touch of his hands that he worked with them. They felt so damn good against her–a little rough and scratchy–and she wished he'd touch her everywhere right now.

"Finn..."

"I know," he said gruffly. "I know. I want it all and I don't know where to begin."

"Losing your pants would be a good start," she teased softly and was relieved when he stood up and did just that. Standing next to the bed in a pair of dark boxer briefs, he was magnificent. His body was exactly as she envisioned, and her mouth actually began to water. Holding out a hand to him, he was back on the bed beside her, his hands lazily skimming up and down her body.

"Your turn," he said thickly, toying with the straps on her bra.

Without breaking eye contact, she reached behind her back to unclasp it, and that's as far as she got because Finn finished peeling it from her body. Her skin felt chilled and heated at the same time until he lowered his head and took one nipple into his mouth and gently suckled.

This just keeps getting better and better...

He licked and kissed first one breast and then the other, and Grace wasn't sure how much more she could take. She never considered herself a foreplay kind of girl, but that was mainly because no man had ever taken his time with it like this. Part of her knew she should lay back and enjoy it, but she wanted more–wanted to explore his body like he was exploring hers. She wanted to touch and taste every inch of him–to find out what he liked, what turned him on. But before her thoughts could go any further, he was moving down her body and taking her panties with him.

Oh, my...

If she thought she was close to having an orgasm before, she was teetering on the edge now. It took less than a minute for her to come apart, crying out his name and she wanted to shout how it wasn't fair–she wanted more–but she needn't have worried. Finn was one step ahead of her.

Lifting his head, he grinned up at her. "More," was all he said, and she was more than willing to oblige.

"Can I ask you something?"

"As long as it doesn't require too many brain cells, sure."

Finn chuckled, his fingers gently playing with her hair. She was curled up beside him, one leg tangled with his and completely naked.

And Grace looked fantastic naked.

She felt even better.

"I know you couldn't get a flight home last night, but... why not fly home today or tomorrow?"

Her hand was tracing small circles on his chest and he felt her slight shrug. "It would have been easy to do–to just grab a hotel room somewhere and all that." Then she let out a mirthless laugh. "I could have made arrangements to get my luggage sent to me too."

When she paused, he didn't push, but he was still curious as hell as to why she'd choose to drive cross country with a stranger when she didn't have to. Finn knew why he was doing it, but he really wanted to hear her story.

"I thought the drive would help me clear my mind or at the very least, help me figure out what the hell I was doing with my life." She moaned. "God, I made such a mess of things."

He really hoped she wasn't referring to him or what they'd just done.

As if reading his mind, she lifted her head and looked at him. "Not this," she clarified, "but with Jared and the wedding." Her hand was resting over his heart, and even though Finn knew he had gone into this tonight knowing it was wrong, right now, he couldn't really believe that.

"You're not the one who made the mess, Grace," he began, but she stopped him.

"I should have gone into that room and confronted both of them and ended things like an adult rather than running away." She rolled away from him and looked up at the ceiling. "The outcome still would have been the same, but...I could have left with at least a sliver of dignity rather than looking like a drowned rat doing some weird version of a walk of shame in a Walmart."

He couldn't help it; the memory of how she looked made him chuckle and she elbowed him in the ribs for it. "Sorry."

"You don't have to be. I looked ridiculous and you have no idea how much that bothers me. I'm not someone who enjoys looking foolish."

That actually surprised him because everything he'd witnessed in the last twenty-four-plus hours told him Grace Mackie was a confident woman who didn't give a damn what anyone thought–which is what he told her.

"It's all a façade," she explained. "In my work as a career coach, I've learned to master the art of always looking confident–never let anyone see you sweat. Fake it till you make it. Blah, blah, blah." She turned her head and looked at him. "I'm really good at what I do. Maybe a little too good."

"What do you mean?"

"I mean, I'm so used to being polished and perfect in front of people that no one can see how I really feel."

Finn rolled onto his side and studied her. "And how do you really feel?"

"Right now?" she said with a sexy grin. "Pretty damn good."

While he appreciated the stroke to his ego, it wasn't what he was looking for. "That's not what I meant."

She groaned. "Okay, fine. I feel like an idiot. Like, how could I have been involved with someone for so long and not known what he was really like?"

He hated to point out the obvious, but... "Maybe you taught him a little too well."

A long, weary sigh was her first response. "That's what I'm afraid of."

There wasn't anything he could say to that because he didn't know her ex, other than the fact that he was a douche who cheated.

Probably not a helpful observation right now.

"So, what happens now?"

She shrugged and rolled onto her side, so they were face to face. "I'm going to have to deal with the aftermath. Luckily, we didn't live together or going home would be a nightmare."

"What kind of aftermath? It seems to me like you two talked things out. If you didn't live together, what else is there?"

Frowning, she was silent for a long moment. "There should be more to it than this, shouldn't there?"

He was afraid to agree or disagree, so he waited her out.

Then she sat up. "You'd think after eighteen months together and canceling a wedding there'd be more to breaking up but…I don't think there is." She turned her head back toward him. "I kept my apartment because it was easier to think about slowly moving into his place–especially after the spur-of-the-moment change of wedding dates." She paused and explained further. "Jared handled all the wedding stuff because it was his idea and a last-minute thing he wanted to do."

Now Finn sat up. "Seriously?"

She nodded. "Yup. I wanted a big family wedding next spring, but Jared insisted we should do this now. I only realized yesterday after hearing his conversation with Steph that he just wanted to secure a promotion." Rolling onto her back again, she flung one arm over her eyes. "Ugh! I'm pathetic!"

Pulling her arm away, he stared down into her face and offered a small smile. "You are *not* pathetic, Grace. He is. You did nothing wrong here."

But she didn't look reassured. "You can't know that, Finn. You don't even know me."

Unfortunately, she was right. Tonight wasn't supposed to be about deep conversations and getting to know each other; it was supposed to be about sex and need and want and then more sex. One night. Did he really want to ruin it by getting all deep and psychological talking about life and the mistakes she made with her ex?

They were going to have plenty of time to talk over the next several days while in the truck together.

Wait, weren't they?

"One more question and then we're done talking," he said, doing his best to keep his distance because what he wanted was to crawl back on top of her and feel her silky limbs wrapped around him again more than anything else.

"O-kay…"

"Now that you've talked to Jared and your family and friends, do you still want to drive all the way to Atlanta, or would you prefer to get on a plane in the morning and head home?" He did his best to keep his tone neutral because he didn't want to sway her. Well, he actually *really* wanted to sway her, but he was trying to be a good guy here and put her needs first.

Yesterday when he had been faced with having to drive cross-country with her, he had been less than enthused, but after spending the day with her–and he wasn't even taking tonight into consideration because this was a temporary reprieve from reality–he found he genuinely liked her. Hell, he wanted to get to know her as a person, as a friend, and as a woman. But if she came to the realization that she needed to go home and get her life in order sooner rather than later, he would take her to the airport in the morning and wish her well.

And then miss her for a really long time.

Maybe forever.

Don't go there...

"Is this your way of saying you want to get rid of me?" And for the first time since he'd met her, she sounded insecure.

He caressed her cheek because he couldn't *not* touch her right now. "That's not what I'm saying at all, Grace. I'm just trying to make sure you're okay."

Her blue eyes stared at him for so long that he wanted to squirm, and then a slow smile appeared on her face. "Just okay?"

He chuckled softly. "Well...maybe a little more than okay."

She nodded. "What's a little more than okay?"

It was clear to see she was relaxed and back to her sassy

self–ready to play and tease him again, and he figured he was more than ready to go along with that as well. "Hmm... more than okay would be...good."

Her grin turned a little wicked. "You want me to be...good?"

That was a loaded question.

"Because good sounds a little...boring," she said, her voice taking on a breathless quality.

Finn's hands skimmed past her jaw, her throat, and landed on her breast, where he used one finger to tease her nipple. "That does sound boring."

"Mmm..."

"How about...I want you to *feel* good," he asked, his own voice going low and gruff. Honestly, he was done playing and talking, but he wanted Grace to be a little desperate and needy for him. "Really, really good."

She purred and squirmed under his touch. "I do. I do feel good, and you have no idea how happy that makes me."

"Happy is good," he agreed, lowering his head and placing a gentle kiss on the nipple he'd just played with. "I really want you to be happy, Grace." He paused. "And naked. I really want you to be happy and naked with me. All the time."

Now he was really done talking. Moving over her, he knew she was feeling the same way because she wrapped herself around him and kissed him with a desperation he knew well because it matched his own.

"Why Albuquerque? Why is that the next stop?" Grace was studying the map on her phone and trying to see what other options there were. They'd been on the road for an hour and Finn was driving the first leg–which was good because all she wanted was another eight hours of sleep. She'd even tried to hammer the point home with today's snarky t-shirt that read "All You Need is Sleep," but no. He hadn't taken the hint. No matter how much she begged for them to stay another day, it didn't work. Besides needing more sleep, she was mildly disappointed since there was still so much she wanted to see and there wasn't time for it. Who knew when she'd ever come back to Vegas, right? And for a brief moment this morning, she'd thought she had convinced him to stay. But then sanity prevailed.

One night, he'd reminded her. Last night had been it. Now they had to get back to reality and back on the road. She'd totally turned down his suggestion of flying home. It would have been super easy, and part of her was a little anxious to see her family and friends and get a little comfort and sympathy from them, but she was also a little anxious to spend more time with Finn and maybe convince him to have at least one more sexy night with her.

Possibly two.

Last night had been...well...it had been a real eye-opener for Grace. Never in her entire sexual life had she felt so thoroughly consumed and satisfied. Not only was Finn an amazing lover–giving and generous and oh-so-yummy–but he showed her just how lacking her sex life had been up until now.

And he thought she was going to be willing to give that up after only one night?

Was he not aware of how freaking good he was in bed?

Something she'd told him repeatedly after every orgasm he gave her and yet he still seemed to cling to the theory that last night was enough.

We'll just see about that, she thought.

But for now, she had to push all sexy thoughts aside and focus on their route. The way he had them going was taking I-40 almost the entire way. It was a twenty-eight-hour drive from Vegas to Atlanta and she knew if they put in some serious time, they could realistically do the drive in two days with both of them alternating every few hours. Something she had mentioned to Finn, but he explained how he didn't want to do more than six to eight hours per day because it was too much time on the road.

And she wasn't completely certain if that was a rule he normally lived by or because it meant being confined in the truck with her.

"You know, I've never done anything like this before," she said, figuring she'd start a conversation.

"Like what? Drive in a truck?" he teased.

"Ha, ha. Very funny. But...yeah. Sort of. We didn't do road trips when I was growing up and any time I've ever traveled, I've flown." And that reminded her... "You know, last night you asked me why I didn't want to fly home from Tahoe, but you never said why you didn't."

She could see the slight tick of his jaw and knew he was fighting with whether or not to answer her.

Which meant it was a story that was either painful or wasn't going to make him look good.

To push or not to push...

"I know you're not afraid of heights," she went on. "We ziplined, rode a roller coaster on top of a hotel, and went on the tallest observation wheel in the country, so...what is it? Hate airport security? Your ears pop too much? C'mon, what's your deal?"

And push it is!

He let out a long breath and didn't take his eyes off the road. "When I was five, my parents took Dave and me on vacation," he began, his voice somber. "We were living up in New York and were flying to Florida to visit my grandparents."

She nodded and waited for him to continue.

"I was pretty excited about the whole thing–first time on a plane and all. And what little boy doesn't want to fly, right?"

She smiled.

"Halfway through the flight, we hit some really bad turbulence. I was so scared that I got sick."

"Oh, no." Reaching out, she patted his hand. "That's not unusual, Finn. It happens all the time. Surely you know that. And you didn't get sick on the coaster last night so... maybe it wouldn't happen if you flew again."

"Yeah, well, I wish that was the end of the story."

"Oh."

"It wasn't one of the big planes, but there were three seats on either side of the aisle. Dave had the window on one side and my mom sat next to him while my dad and I were on the other side so I could have that window seat. An elderly gentleman was sitting next to my dad. He laughed when I got sick, called me a wimp."

Damn, now she felt bad for making him talk about this.

"Anyway, my dad told him to shut up and helped me get cleaned up. And I remember thinking how much I hated that guy for making fun of me and I hoped he got sick. So when we hit another patch of turbulence, I glared at him and almost willed him to get sick."

"And did he?"

Finn nodded grimly. "Had a heart attack and died right there in the seat." He shuddered. "It was a full flight and we were already making our approach to the airport and there wasn't anything anyone could do. We just had to sit there next to him. I freaked out–like majorly freaked out. When our vacation was over, I refused to get on the plane to go home. My mom and Dave flew, but my dad rented a car and drove us home." He paused. "I haven't flown since."

"Holy shit."

He nodded. "Yup."

"I...wow...I don't even know what to say, Finn. I'm so sorry." And she truly was. Not only because it happened to him at such a young age, but how it was clearly still affecting him today. And honestly, how could it not? That sounded pretty traumatic. And to have it happen on his very first flight? Um...yeah. She could totally understand his hesitation to get on a plane. "Have you even tried...?"

"Nope."

"Would you ever try...?"

"Nope."

Okay, then. He was clearly a man of conviction–or completely stubborn–depending on how you wanted to look at it. And rather than debate that with him or even keep him thinking about such a traumatic event in his life, Grace knew she needed to change gears.

"So yeah, no road trips for me," she said cheerily. "I guess we could say I'm a road trip virgin, huh?"

He didn't acknowledge that.

"Who knew I could be a virgin of anything at twenty-eight, right?" she asked with a laugh.

Nothing.

With a sigh, she returned her attention to her phone to try to see if there was going to be anything exciting to see when they stopped in Albuquerque for the night. Finn's rigid driving schedule would put them stopping for the night at around five–which could realistically give them at least a few hours to explore. And if she was going to do this whole road trip thing, she wanted to see more than just the interstate.

"Oh, my gosh, Finn!" she exclaimed, slapping a hand against his arm. "Did you know Albuquerque is known as the Hot Air Ballooning Capital of the World?" She looked over at him. "Do you think we could ride in a hot air balloon tonight, maybe before dinner or something?"

He merely glanced over at her and shook his head. "Grace, you realize this isn't a vacation, right? We're trying to get home."

And something in his tone seriously irked her. "Really? Are you sure? Because if you were so anxious to get home, you wouldn't have us stopping for the night at five in the afternoon. I mean, that's the time senior citizens go to dinner, Finn! They consider that to be late even though they're called early bird dinners! You realize you're essentially a thirty-year-old senior citizen, right?"

His knuckles were white as he gripped the steering wheel harder and it just made her want to poke at him a little more. "I get that you don't want either of us feeling sleepy behind the wheel, but if we're going to stop so early, I don't see why we can't go out and explore a bit. These places are all new to me and I just thought it would be a fun way to pass the time, that's all."

"Really? That's all? I don't know about you, but I don't have a bottomless budget for this trip. I don't believe in just throwing my money away. I work very hard for what I have, and last night was as frivolous as I want to be on this return trip, so...no. I don't think we can ride in a hot air balloon tonight. At least I can't. If you want to go do it, then be my guest."

Grace thought her jaw just might be on the floor because...wow. Talk about extremes. What happened to the man who rocked her world last night? Where was the guy who was wild and playful and downright wicked on the High Roller?

Then it hit her–this was all part of his plan to put them back on track. She would have appreciated it if he wasn't being such a colossal jerk. It was one thing to try to keep the conversation neutral; it was quite another to just be rude. Fun Finn was gone and in his place was the boring and practical guy that no one would want to hang out with.

No wonder Dave stole his car.

"Can I ask you something?" she said after a minute and realized this was becoming a thing with them. Most of their conversations started with that same question.

"Sure."

"What did you and Dave argue about before he borrowed your car?" She purposely said *borrowed* to get a rise out of him.

"Stole, not borrowed. *Stole*. Dave *stole* my car," he corrected, and Grace had to fight a grin.

"Yeah, whatever. To-mato, to-mahto. He has your car and you don't. Why?"

He shot her another glare before answering. "My brother is a screwup," he stated firmly. "He's constantly going from job to job and none of them pay well, which means he's constantly mooching off our parents. I'd like for them to have a little time to themselves and some financial security when it's time for them to retire, and that's never going to happen unless Dave gets his shit together."

Again...wow.

"He went to college, had every opportunity, and he's still like a child who can't decide what he wants to be when he grows up!" He shook his head. "He's gone through so many jobs and most of them, I helped him get. Then he screws up and gets fired and you know who looks bad? Me! I mean, I keep trying to help him and he keeps screwing me!"

"And you took this trip with him...why?"

"I thought we'd spend some time together and could bond a bit, and maybe I could figure out where his head is at so I could help him find steady employment." He shook his head. "But it's impossible because all Dave wants to do is party and have fun and not have any responsibility! Why is it okay for him to be a slack-ass, huh? Everyone else works and supports themselves. Why does he think he doesn't have to? I've been working since I was fifteen years old. Fifteen! I own a business. I own my house. My parents aren't giving *me* any money and I wouldn't ask them to!"

So...here was a can of worms she couldn't possibly cram back where they came from.

"Finn, maybe he just..."

"No, he's always been like this–like the rules of the world don't apply to him! He's the typical baby of the family. Everyone should cater to Dave. No one hurt Dave's feelings," he mocked. "It's ridiculous. He's a grown man and should act like one."

"Well, sure, but..."

"Do you think I want to get up and work ten hours a day, six days a week?" he snapped.

"I...I don't know. You seem like..."

"Because I don't! Sometimes I'd like to just kick back and take a day off, but I don't. You think I don't want to just go off and ride in a freaking hot air balloon and just forget about all of my responsibilities? Because I would love to! But I can't! This trip was the first vacation I've had in years. *Years!* And look what happened? I should have just minded my own business and stayed at the shop and let my parents handle Dave!"

That was it. She'd had enough.

It was time for someone to kick Mr. Martyr in the ass and knock some sense into him.

"I'm sorry, but why *aren't* your parents the ones handling Dave?" she asked sarcastically. "Seems to me he's *their* son, *their* responsibility, not yours, Finn! And you know what? Maybe it wouldn't be the worst thing in the world for all of you to just let him fail at something! You should probably tell your folks that, too. Although this is all going to be a moot point when he gets back to Atlanta in a stolen car and gets arrested, so...problem solved." She crossed her arms over her chest for emphasis.

Finn slammed on the breaks, and Grace wanted to think it was in outrage over her suggestion, but she realized there was traffic and everyone was suddenly at a standstill.

"Are you out of your mind, Grace?" he demanded. "That's your solution to this? Have him arrested? Let jail teach Dave a lesson? Isn't that a little heartless?"

It would be comical if his reaction wasn't so damn sad. Twisting in her seat, she gave him a hard look. "You have to pick a side here, Finn," she began calmly. "You want to teach him a lesson, but you don't want him to face any consequences for his poor decisions. Then you're mad at the decisions he makes and don't like the punishment he gets. I mean...come on! Can't you see how you're just enabling the entire situation?"

He waved her off. "You don't know what you're talking about."

"I may not know enough about your family dynamic to say with any kind of certainty, but I can tell by what you're saying that *you're* part of the problem!"

"I'm...*what?*" He slammed his hands on the steering wheel. "That's it. You're completely unreasonable. We're not talking about this anymore!"

"Why not? We have nothing else to do! We're stuck here in traffic and we're having a conversation! It's not my fault you can't handle a little criticism!"

"I handle criticism just fine when it's accurate," he argued. "Don't sit there and play armchair psychologist with me, Grace. You're only making yourself look bad."

Lucky for him she wasn't a violent person because right now she was tempted to punch him in the throat. However, she also had two older brothers who taught her how to play a little dirty and retaliate without getting physical.

"Fine. I can handle that. Unlike you." She paused for a second. "I mean, as an adult, I can sit here and take you disagreeing with my opinion. It's a shame you can't do the same."

She thought his head was going to explode. But to his credit, he didn't say a word to her.

Not. One. Word.

Fine. He wanted to block her out and pretend she wasn't even here? Well, two could play this game.

He was stubborn, of that there was no doubt, but she was about to prove he was no match for her. Reaching into her satchel, she pulled out her iPod. If Finn wanted to be a jerk, then that was fine with her. It wasn't going to ruin her day. Sticking her earbuds in, she was more than ready to listen to something other than his warped view of his family relationship. Scrolling through her playlists, she picked her most upbeat one, hit play, and began to sing.

Loudly.

Bruno Mars' *Uptown Funk* was the first song, and not

only was she going to sing along, but she was an expert at passenger seat choreography.

Out of the corner of her eye, she could see Finn sitting there fuming.

Good.

Game on.

6

By the time they pulled into the hotel parking lot at six p.m., Finn was ready to lose his mind. He thought chatty Grace was going to be a problem, but that was *nothing* compared to the spectacle of singing and dancing Grace he'd been stuck with for the last several hours. Once the traffic hit and she stopped talking to him, it was like nothing he'd ever experienced before.

Now I know what hell feels like...

They had pulled off the interstate to gas up, grab some fast food, and switch positions. Finn thought she'd possibly give up the singing and definitely give up the dancing. Hell, he even figured they had played the silent game long enough and they'd resume some conversation.

He was wrong, though.

So very, very wrong.

He lost count of how many times he'd shouted for her to put both hands on the steering wheel and stop with the ridiculous dance moves, but with her earbuds in, she hadn't heard him. Then he reminded her how driving with earbuds in was illegal, so she'd simply plugged her iPod into the car's USB and let her music play through the sound system.

Loudly.

It would have been pointless to argue that he didn't enjoy her music and that she was being incredibly inconsiderate and borderline rude because *clearly,* that was exactly what she was trying to do.

In all his arguments with his brother, neither had ever done anything quite so childish.

Then again, he could argue that in all his arguments with Grace, she hadn't stolen his car and left him stranded.

Yet.

And dammit, now *that* thought was in his head. What if she was so pissed off at him that she took off without him tomorrow? The truck was rented in her name and her name only. Why hadn't he agreed to put his name on the rental agreement when he was asked about it? Groaning, he had to think of a way to make sure she wouldn't leave him without putting the idea in her head if it wasn't there already.

She parked the truck and climbed out without a word, and he was relieved that the music finally stopped. Holy crap! How could one person listen to so much dance music? Finn didn't think people even listened to Britney Spears anymore, but obviously, Grace did!

He climbed out and stalked after her into the lobby. They didn't make any reservations in advance; they'd just planned on getting into town and finding someplace to stay for the night then.

"Hey!" Grace said cheerily to the guy behind the desk. "I need a room for tonight, please!"

The guy eyed him and then looked back at Grace with a smile. "Just one night?"

"Yup!"

"And...just one room?"

Finn rolled his eyes and could almost guarantee she was batting her eyes at the guy.

"Just one, Mark," she said sweetly. "Oh, and if you have something far away from an elevator, that would be perfect. I hate the noise."

Mark smiled back at her. "I'm not sure I can do that. We've got a convention here in town and we don't have a lot of vacancies..."

Finn's stomach sank. He had a feeling he knew what was coming next.

"But you've got the last one!" Mark said happily. "It's not right next to an elevator, but you're only three rooms down. I hope that's okay."

"It will be fine. Thank you!"

Behind her, Finn fumed. Now what? What the hell was *he* supposed to do? Then he figured they'd just have to share the room again like last night. Well, obviously not exactly like last night, but...

Grace looked over her shoulder at him. "I think there was another hotel across the street if you want to try over there."

Hell no...

Mark looked up at the two of them, and Finn forced himself to smile. He stepped in close and wrapped one hand around her arm, speaking low, "Can I speak to you for a minute, Grace?"

She tried to pull away but seemed to think better of making a scene. When they were out of earshot, he did his best to remain calm. "There is no way I'm going across the street or anyplace else tonight," he hissed. "If there's only one room, then we're sharing it."

Her eyes went wide before narrowing at him. "Oh, really?" she asked sarcastically. "Well, I don't think so. Not after you were such a colossal jerk today! If you don't want to go to another hotel, then you can sleep in the truck!"

Oh, it was tempting. If he did, then he could guarantee she couldn't leave without him, but then...

He'd be sleeping in a truck.

No. Just no.

The only way to get around this was to apologize. He knew it and hoped she'd be gracious enough to do the same.

"Listen, Grace, I think we can both agree things got a little...well...a little out of control. I'm sorry. I snapped at you and that was wrong, okay? The subject of my family is... well...it's a touchy thing."

"Pfft...no kidding," she said, rolling her eyes and crossing her arms over her chest again.

He had to remind himself that he was trying to make nice right now. "Okay, I get it. I was a jerk, but you have to admit you were just as bad! All that ridiculous dancing and singing and..."

"Oh, so now happy and upbeat music is bad too? Where does it end?" she said dramatically. "Is the sky too blue for you? The sun too bright? Children's laughter get on your nerves too?"

If she was trying to push his every last button and make his head explode, she was succeeding.

"Miss Mackie?" Mark called out from the desk. Grace looked over at him and then back to Finn.

"You said we needed to go back to normal today. Well, normal means no sharing rooms."

"No," he corrected, "normal means not sharing a bed." And just saying the word while standing this close to her had him wanting to reconsider that too. She seriously drove him crazy, and right now, he'd like nothing more than to take her up to the room, throw her down on the bed, and return the favor.

Mark called her name again and he could see the indecision on her face, but it was brief. "Fine," she murmured. "Just...try not to be a jerk again." Walking all of three steps away, she murmured over her shoulder, "If that's even possible."

He was smart enough to keep his mouth shut and simply follow her to get the room key. "You want to grab the bags now or after dinner?" he asked after a minute.

"I guess now. I know I showered this morning, and these are clean clothes, but the thought of freshening up is pretty damn exciting." She walked out to the parking lot ahead of him and now all he could think about was Grace in the shower–naked and sudsy and so damn appealing.

It was going to be a long night.

"I'm so full. I can't walk."

"Then we're both screwed because...I'm too full to walk."

They were sitting in a Mexican restaurant with the remnants of their meal between them, which consisted of way too much chips and salsa.

Followed by queso and guacamole.

"It was like they were never going to end," Grace said, sitting back in her chair with her hand on her belly. "Every time I thought we were done, they just brought out more."

"We could have asked them to stop."

She glared at him. "But they were so good! Why would you want that to stop?"

And her mind immediately went to the gutter, with

images of all the things they did the night before and how good *they* were and how she didn't want them to stop.

"Because now we're going to have to live here because we're too full to leave," he said, pulling her from her dirty thoughts. "And no doubt the chips and salsa and guac will just keep coming. It'll be like some sort of delicious yet vicious cycle."

"I'm glad we're not going up in a hot air balloon after this. I'd hate to have to hurl all over the city," she said, chuckling softly. "Oh...it even hurts to laugh."

"Would you like to see a dessert menu?" their waiter asked, smiling.

"NO!" they said in unison, and the poor guy quickly excused himself.

"You think we scared him?" Finn asked, laughing. "Damn, you're right. It does hurt to laugh."

"Told you so." She was too full and uncomfortable to enjoy the fact that he stuck his tongue out at her. It was nice to see his sense of humor was returning a bit. Although, after they had checked into their room and relaxed a little, she felt like they were back on an even keel. There were two beds in the room–she wasn't sure if she was happy or sad about that–and they each claimed one and watched some TV before freshening up and heading to get something to eat that wasn't served in a paper bag.

She understood Finn's earlier comments about a budget for this trip. Honestly, she didn't have much of a disposable income either. She made a good living as a career coach, but if she was going to spend money on a getaway, this certainly wasn't it. Last night's expenses were easy because she'd won on the slot machine. If she hadn't, chances were she would have been happy just walking around and seeing everything rather than actually doing everything.

She groaned.

"You okay?"

Nodding, Grace thought it was safer not to bring up all the things they did last night. As it was, she was curious about how it was going to be when they got back to the room. It was one thing to say it would be cool and fine and not at all awkward, but knowing Finn was sleeping only a few feet away, it was going to be a hard temptation to resist.

Really hard.

Across from her, he stretched and slowly stood, groaning with each movement.

Okay, maybe resisting him wouldn't be so hard. After all, if one Mexican meal could bring him down like this and have him groaning like an old man, how could she possibly find that sexy, right?

He stretched again, and his t-shirt rode up, exposing a thin band of skin across his flat stomach and her thoughts of old men were instantly pushed aside.

There was her dessert. Six feet of yumminess.

"You ready to go?" he asked, once again breaking into her thoughts.

"Sure." Slowing coming to her feet, she now understood all his groaning. She was sure that he was thinking unsexy thoughts about her too. They paid their tab by the front door and walked slowly back to the hotel. The restaurant was only two blocks away and it seemed silly to drive.

At least, it seemed silly before they ate their weight in tacos.

"Did you want to do some sightseeing?" Finn asked casually as they walked along the sidewalk.

"I know I should say yes because who knows when I'll ever come back here, but I think I just want to go back to the room, put on my jammies, and sleep this food baby off."

Beside her, he chuckled. "Food baby?"

She patted her belly. "Yup. I've named her Nacho Belle." They both laughed, and without realizing it, they were holding hands. Grace didn't pull her hand away and she couldn't be sure if Finn was aware they were doing it, but she liked it. A lot. "What about you?"

He looked down at his stomach. "I don't think, as a man, I can claim a food baby."

Laughing, she shook her head. "No! Although that is really funny. I meant, did you want to go sightseeing?"

He shook his head. "Nah. I've been here before, and honestly, I'm beat. The thought of just hanging out and watching TV until I fall asleep sounds pretty much perfect right now."

"I hate to agree, but...I agree."

"Why hate?"

"Like I said, I've never been to Albuquerque before, and even though we can't ride a hot air balloon, there seemed to be a lot of cool things to do and see."

"Grace..."

"Yeah, yeah, yeah. I know. This isn't a vacation or a pleasure trip. No unlimited budget. Blah, blah, blah. I remember," she muttered.

"That wasn't what I was going to say."

Somehow she doubted that, but for now, she'd humor him. "Really?"

He nodded. "Really."

"Then what were you going to say?"

"I was going to say we can make it an early night but maybe get up early tomorrow and see some sights. What do you think?"

She thought he was being incredibly sweet, and now she felt bad for mocking him in her head.

And out loud.

She squeezed his hand. "That sounds good. Thanks." Pausing for a moment, she thought about some of the things she read online earlier. "I should probably do a little more research tonight so we get to see some of the important stuff and don't waste time."

He nodded again. "Sure. Sounds like a plan."

They walked the rest of the way in silence and stayed that way until they were back in their room. Finn asked if she would mind if he showered first, and she was more than willing to let him since she was still painfully full. While he was in there, Grace pulled out her phone and checked in with her mother.

"Grace! Sweetheart, I really wish you would fly home and be done with this," her mother said, her voice full of concern. "I hate how you're dealing with this by yourself and driving all alone. It's not safe!"

Yeah, she hadn't mentioned Finn and their arrangement to anyone.

"I'm fine, Mom. I promise. I just really need this time to get my head together." Sighing, she reclined against the pillows on her bed.

"There's nothing wrong with your head, sweetheart."

"Yeah, well...you're supposed to say that. You're my mother."

"Yes, well, that's true, but it's not the only reason I'm saying it." She paused. "If you want to know the truth, we're all a little relieved you didn't marry Jared."

She sat straight up at her mother's words. "What? Why would you even say that? I thought everyone liked Jared!"

"Like is a strong word..."

"Mom..."

"Okay, look. You loved him, and we all...well...we *tried*

to love him too. But Jared wasn't particularly lovable. And I hate saying this because I don't want to be accused of bashing him and then you get back together and things get awkward."

"Believe me, we will *not* be getting back together. Like ever. You have my guarantee on that."

"Still, I don't like to do things like this. You know I rarely speak ill of anyone."

If Grace knew one thing about her mother, it was that she never liked to criticize anyone, so the fact that she was sharing her feelings like this right now meant she was serious. "Why didn't you ever say anything?"

"Because I wasn't the one who was going to be married to him!" she said with a small laugh. "You're an excellent judge of character and I figured you saw something in him I didn't. It's not as important for your family to love the one you marry as it is for you to love them."

Sighing, she lay back down. "What if...what if I said I wasn't sure I was ever really in love with him?"

"I'd say right now you're lashing out because you're hurt," her mother said sympathetically. "And that's okay. You don't have to say you never loved him because you think loving someone who betrayed you is a bad thing. Every relationship–even failed ones–are a good thing. They help us grow and figure out what we want and who we are. I'm just sorry it ended the way it did, Grace. I hate that no one was there for you."

"No one to blame but me for that," she said quietly.

"Grace," her mother began sympathetically, "that's not the way it was."

She let out a mirthless laugh. "You're being far too gracious." Then she paused. "And...you know...it's not really lashing out, Mom. I'd been having doubts for a while, and I think he knew, and it was why he wanted to rush the wedding." Another mirthless laugh. "Of course, now I know there were other factors involved too, but still. We'd been growing apart and he was...oh, God, he was just so exhausting! Everything was about him! We never did the things I wanted to do or hung out with the people I wanted to hang out with!"

"Then why did you stay?"

"Honestly? I thought it would get better. I kept thinking if he got the promotion, he'd chill out, and once we got married, it would be one less thing on our plate to stress about." She groaned. "Some of my friends talked about how stressed they were from planning a wedding, and I figured that added to the whole thing as well. And in the end, look what happened! I can't believe I let Jared talk me into changing everything and I went along with it knowing you and Dad and everyone who mattered to me wouldn't be there."

"Well, we were still having a reception..."

"Mom, don't. It was incredibly selfish of me to do this and...and I feel like I got what I deserved."

"Oh, sweetie, no! Don't say that! I looked at it like you and Jared were eloping, but it was planned well in advance," she said with a laugh. "Trust me, your father and I were a little relieved not to have to pay for a full-blown wedding. Your sister broke the bank on hers and you know we helped both your brothers too. So maybe if *we* hadn't been so selfish..."

"Oh, my gosh! Stop!" she cried. "Mom, I love how you always try to see the bright side of things, but sometimes it's okay to admit that someone did something wrong! I did–I did something wrong! And it was selfish and completely inconsiderate, and I'm sorry. For everything. My whole life, when I envisioned my wedding, you and Dad were always there. Always! I've even mocked people who were selfish enough to get married without their families there and look what I went and almost did! I'm so sorry I let Jared talk me into giving up my dream wedding."

Her mother was quiet for a moment and Grace was pretty sure she heard a small sob. "Never let anyone take away your dreams, baby girl. I'm so sorry you're hurting and alone, and I promise when you get home, your father and I are going to take care of you and whatever you need, okay?"

"You don't have to do that, Mom."

"You're our baby and it's what we love to do. Ask any parent and they'll tell you the same thing."

"I'm a little old for that sort of thing. I'm a grown woman and I need to be able to take care of myself."

A soft sigh was the first response she heard. "Let me tell you something, and I want you to remember this because someday you'll feel the same way too."

"O-kay..."

"You never stop being a parent, Grace. It doesn't matter how old you get; you are always going to be my daughter. My little girl. And when you hurt, I hurt. If there is something I can do to comfort you or help you or...or anything, then I'm going to do it. Do you understand?"

Nodding, she fought back the tears. "Thanks, Mom. I needed to hear that."

"Good." There was relief in her voice. "Is the hotel you're at in a good neighborhood? Is it safe? Have you bolted the door?"

She laughed softly and, in the distance, heard Finn was out of the shower. "Everything is fine here and I'm in a very good neighborhood, so please don't worry. I promise to call and check in tomorrow, okay?"

"Yes, please do and be safe!"

"I will, Mom. I love you."

"Love you too."

Grace shut her phone down and placed it on the mattress beside her, her eyes stinging with unshed tears. "God, what a mess," she whispered and suddenly wished she was at home with her folks. Right now, she could use one of her father's famous hugs and a slice of her mother's apple pie. The thought of food made her stomach lurch a bit, but it passed quickly.

The room was getting darker and when she looked toward the window, she saw the clouds moving in and knew they were in for some rain.

"Fits my mood," she murmured, as the tears began to roll down her face. At the sound of a door opening, she quickly wiped them away as she sat up.

Finn stepped out of the bathroom in a pair of jeans and nothing else. His hair was damp, and even from across the room, she could see several droplets of water on his chest and had to fight the urge to get up and lick them.

Bad Grace!

"Bathroom's all yours," he said with an easy grin. "Water gets hot fast, so be careful, and the pressure is great."

Before she gave in to the temptation to simply body slam him to the nearest bed and taste him, she grabbed her things and with a mumbled word of thanks, stepped into the steamy room and closed the door behind her.

It wasn't like Finn wasn't aware of how long some women took to get ready, but it seemed like Grace was taking an exorbitant amount of time in the shower. She hadn't been that way this morning before they left Vegas, so he had to wonder what the deal was now.

Was she regretting the fact they were sharing a room tonight? Platonically? Hell, if he were honest, he could admit he kind of was. If things had gone as planned, he'd be in a room all by himself, wishing he could be with Grace but knowing it was for the best for them to be in separate rooms.

Yeah. That had to be what it was. She was just killing as much time as possible so they didn't have to lie in separate beds, mere feet away, and pretend they hadn't seen each other naked and touched every inch of each other only twenty-four hours ago.

Then he remembered the look on her face when he'd come out of the bathroom. She looked upset and on the verge of tears. He heard part of her conversation with her mother and he imagined she was a little emotional from that. He just wished she didn't feel like she had to hide out in the bathroom instead of showing her feelings out here or even talking to him about them.

And why do you think that is?

Okay, fine. He hadn't been the nicest guy in the world today, but they were over that, right? Everyone was entitled to a bit of a meltdown considering the circumstances, and he had his, and it was done. He was going to move on just like he always did, and...unfortunately, he had no idea how Grace handled bad days or bad situations.

Other than getting in an Uber and taking off in a wedding dress, that is.

A loud boom of thunder sounded and he jumped a little. They were getting one hell of a storm, and personally, he was glad they weren't out there driving in it. Of course, they would have been about a hundred miles away by now, but still, he was happy to be off the road and relaxing in a room.

The curtains were drawn, and he had stripped out of his jeans and was currently under the sheets in just his boxers flipping through the channels. When Grace finally came out of the bathroom, he almost forgot how to breathe.

The electric blue nightshirt matched her eyes and barely covered her ass. She didn't have on a stitch of makeup, her hair was damp, and she was quite possibly even sexier than she'd been last night in scraps of red silk.

She gave him a weak smile as she walked over to her bed to pull down the covers. When she bent over, he caught a glimpse of blue panties that matched her nightshirt, and he knew it wasn't a deliberate move.

"Hey," he said softly, reaching out a hand to her.

She stopped what she was doing and turned to look at him. "Hmm?"

Then he did something he had no intention of doing. He slid a little farther across the bed and gently tugged her toward him until she had one knee on the bed.

"Finn..."

But he was already shaking his head. "Come here." She crawled onto the bed and positioned herself next to him until he could put his arms around her, and then he simply held her. "You just looked like you needed a hug."

He thought he was doing a good thing, but she broke down sobbing in his arms.

So he held her a little tighter.

And she cried a little bit harder.

After a few minutes, she raised her head and looked at him. "How did you know?"

He could be honest, or he could try to make her laugh.

He decided to do both.

"Well, you looked a little sad after talking to your mom," he began, "but then the four-hour shower really gave it away."

She chuckled and wiped at her eyes. "Four hours? Exaggerate much?"

"I never exaggerate about time," he corrected. "Inches, yes. Time, no."

Then she really started to laugh, but she hugged him tightly. "Thank you. You have no idea how much I needed that."

Finn realized there was a lot he didn't know about Grace, but in the short time they'd spent together, he also knew he'd learned a lot. When she went to move out of his arms, he held her close. If she would have turned and asked him why he wasn't letting her go, he wasn't sure what he'd say, but luckily, she didn't question him. They simply shifted and got a little more comfortable. "Seriously, are you okay?"

"Yeah, I think so. I'm probably going to be like this for a while–fine one minute, a weepy, sobbing mess the next." She shook her head. "Be thankful you only have another couple of days of this to deal with."

There were many things in this world that Finn was thankful for; saying goodbye to Grace wasn't going to be one of them.

Guiding her head onto his shoulder, he felt her shuddery sigh. "Right before you came out of the bathroom earlier, I wished I was home with my parents. They always make me feel better. I'm the baby of the family and Mom was just reminding me of all the ways she and my dad would take care of me when I got home."

There was sadness and longing in her voice and Finn

reminded her of her options. "We can book you a flight right now," he said quietly. "I'm sure there are flights out of here first thing in the morning. You could be home with them by lunchtime tomorrow."

She was quiet for so long that Finn wasn't sure she heard him, but when she pulled back and looked at him, he knew she had. He just couldn't tell what she was thinking.

"Do you think I should?"

No fair, he thought. None of this was fair. How could he possibly meet a woman who was sweet and funny and sexy and attractive and completely annoying and have her here half-naked in his bed when he knew he was going to have to let her go? Everything was against them—everything. Between where they lived and the timing of when they met, it just didn't make sense.

But man, oh man, did he want it to.

Swallowing hard, he struggled for the right words. "That's not for me to decide, Grace. You need to do what's right for you."

Pushing away slightly, she growled, and he knew it was meant to show her frustration, but it just came out sounding kind of cute and really sexy.

Actually, she had made that sound a time or two last night while they were naked and sweaty and trying to consume each other.

Focus, dammit!

"If I knew what was right for me, I wouldn't be in this predicament right now, Finn! I think we can both agree that I *suck* at making decisions like this, so can you please not give me the politically correct answer and just tell me what I should do?"

"Grace, I..."

"You seem to enjoy being the boss, being the one in

control, so can you please just...do that right now? Do I hop on a plane and go home, or do I take some time away from everything and try to get my head on straight for a few more days?"

Honestly, he had no idea which response she wanted from him, so he stayed quiet. When he didn't respond, she pushed a little more. "Pretend I'm your brother! You obviously like telling *him* what to do! Only in this scenario, I'm the baby and the screwup! I'm the one who's the drain on the family! So come on, what do I do?"

And for some reason, the comparison bothered him—*really* bothered him. "I'm not going to even try to compare you and Dave..."

"Why? Because I'm a woman?"

He rolled his eyes. "No, because you are *not* a screwup, Grace! You were in a shitty situation and you're dealing with it. Dave makes every situation shitty and expects everyone else to deal with it and fix it, so..."

She jumped up and onto her knees. "Fine! So don't fixate on the comparison! Fixate on helping me decide what I'm supposed to do! Again, am I supposed to book a flight home for tomorrow morning so I can be comforted by my family, or am I supposed to take this ride across the rest of the country and embrace the time to get my head together? There are only two choices here, Finn! Surely out of the two of us, you can pick the right option!"

It was on the tip of his tongue to throw a third option out there—to stay on this trip because she wanted to spend time with him and explore what was happening between them.

But he didn't.

Tears welled up in her eyes and he forced himself to look away. It was a total dick move—he was pretty much being a coward—but this decision was no easier for him than it was for her. And if he said that to her—if he admitted he was struggling too—then where would they be? How could that possibly help anything?

He could feel her staring at him—waiting for an answer or at the very least, an acknowledgment of her question. So many thoughts swirled around in his mind, and for a long moment, fear held him paralyzed. Never in his life had he been faced with a predicament like this. The practical side of him said he should convince her to get on the first plane out in the morning and let that be it. But for the first time in his life, his heart was telling him to be reckless—that sometimes what seemed logical and practical wasn't necessarily the right choice.

It was a hell of a situation to find himself in.

She shoved him hard, her voice laced with disgust. "Damn you."

As she went to move off the bed, he decided to listen to his heart. He had nothing else to lose. He was done fighting how he felt. This might not solve anything, but he'd gain some peace of mind by getting it off his chest. Grabbing her arm, he tugged her close again, and Grace clumsily sprawled across his lap. "Don't book a flight. Don't go home yet. Stay with me, finish the drive with me." He reached up and anchored a hand in her hair. "Sing to music I can't stand, dance in your seat all you want and ask to stop at every tacky roadside attraction, just...don't go." He rested his forehead against hers. "Not yet." He was breathless by the time he was done talking, and when he could finally breathe, he pulled back slightly and looked at her.

And saw her smile.

"You don't want me to go."

He shook his head. "I don't want you to go."

Her smile grew. "Tomorrow, can we listen to the hair bands of the eighties while we drive?" she asked, straightening and then crawling over him until she was straddling his lap. "I have a fantastic playlist with bands like Whitesnake, Def Leppard, Mötley Crüe, and Poison."

Finn's hands moved down until they rested on her ass and he gently squeezed. "Do I have to headbang with you or can I just drive?"

"A little air guitar wouldn't hurt."

"I always envisioned myself more of a drummer."

"That'll work," she said, her voice a little soft and husky. "You have really good hands. I think you'd make a great drummer."

With a short laugh, he pulled her in close. "You think so, huh?"

Nodding, she replied, "I know so. Think you'll be able to drum and drive?"

Now wasn't the time to remind her–again–of the dangers of that sort of thing, so he simply said, "I think I can handle that." Leaning in close, he was hoping to kiss her, but she reared back. "Grace?"

With a sexy grin, she pulled her nightshirt up and over her head, tossing it to the floor. "Think you can handle this too?"

His hands instantly moved to cup her breasts, and as he lowered his lips to them, he replied, "I'll handle whatever it is you need me to, Grace."

And he would.

7

THEY HAD JUST SWITCHED places in Amarillo when Finn realized this trip was good for him too. He was learning to compromise a little more, to be more flexible with his schedule, and to be spontaneous.

That last one wasn't nearly as painful as he thought it would be.

They didn't leave the hotel this morning at the time he had originally planned. Grace had started the day by making him laugh wearing a t-shirt that said "You Had Me at Tacos," and they commiserated over how much they ate the night before. Once they stopped laughing, she had insisted on going for pancakes for breakfast. And he had to admit, he was glad they did that because the pancakes were delicious. And even though neither of them should have been hungry again between last night's dinner and this morning's breakfast, they had stopped to eat again here in Amarillo. She'd convinced him to stop at what he could only describe as a dive, but he had to admit the food–Texas barbecue–was awesome.

"You know," he began, settling into the passenger seat,

"I have us stopping in Oklahoma City for the night, but if you want to stop someplace else..."

Grace looked over at him and smiled happily. "That's very sweet of you, but I was doing my research while you were driving, and now I'm looking forward to checking it out. Why? Was there someplace else you'd rather stop?"

"I'm so tired that I wouldn't mind staying here in Amarillo," he replied lightly, and he was only partially kidding. After Grace had crawled into his lap last night, they made love twice before dozing off. Then she woke him up around three in the morning and he made love to her again.

And again when the alarm went off at seven.

That, combined with their lack of sleep from the night before in Vegas, and he was lucky he could see straight.

Beside him, she chuckled softly. "I hate to say it, but we definitely need to sleep tonight."

"Are you sure you're okay to drive? Because if you're too tired, we can totally find a place to stop now. Maybe even nap for a couple of hours and then drive through the night."

She was quiet as she pulled out onto the highway. They drove less than a mile before she glanced over at him. "Here's something you should know about me–I hate driving at night. Like seriously hate it. I will drive all day long, but once the sun goes down, I prefer not to be the designated driver. That's why your schedule has worked so well."

"Is there a reason for that–for why you don't like driving at night?"

"Promise not to laugh?"

He nodded.

"I'm normally an early-to-bed kind of girl," she said shyly. "All of my friends tease me and call me the eleven-thirty woman because I am never out later than that, and if

I'm home, I'm always asleep by then." Grinning at him, she added, "I know you wouldn't know it based on the last couple of days, but...there it is."

Was it wrong that her little fact only made her more attractive? Why? Because he was an early-to-bed kind of guy. Granted, his early mornings at the shop sort of dictated that, but still, Finn didn't know too many people his age who had the same habit.

"See? No laughing," he said.

"Well, I appreciate it. I get made fun of a lot because of it. When most of my friends are just heading out on a Friday night, I'm already in my jammies and curling up with a book."

He really wouldn't have pegged her for that, especially after their romp around Vegas. She seemed like...

Turning his head, Finn looked at her. "Did your feet really hurt in Vegas or were you really just looking to make it an early night?"

"You do realize it was almost two in the morning at that point, right?"

He nodded. "I know, but...still. Were you just tired?"

Her smile was back. "You really want to know?"

He nodded.

"The shoes were new and mildly uncomfortable, but my real reason for wanting to go back to the room was all about seducing you." Now her grin was of pure satisfaction. "And it was better than I ever imagined."

Groaning, Finn rested his head back against the seat. "I really wish you hadn't told me that."

"Why? I would have thought you'd appreciate the compliment."

"Oh, I do. Believe me. But that's not what I was talking about."

"Then...why?"

"Because now I'm going to have to find out where the nearest hotel is for us to stop," he said gruffly. "Knowing you did that for me? It's a huge turn on and I'd like to properly thank you."

Giggling, Grace sped up a bit and passed the slow-moving Ford in front of them and then whipped off the next exit. She looked over at him and winked. "I already saw the sign a minute ago and was thinking about surprising you again."

This girl.

It was one in the afternoon, they had eaten before leaving Amarillo–all of fifteen minutes ago–and they were already stopping again. Normally, this sort of thing made Finn crazy. On the trip west with his brother, any time Dave tried to sway him from his schedule, Finn lectured on why it was important to stick to it.

Then again, Dave was his brother and not an incredibly sexy and desirable woman who Finn was only going to have a few more days with. He wanted to cram as much as possible into their time together–whether it be sex or sightseeing.

But right now, he was really happy it was for sex.

Like really, really happy.

He realized how crazy that was considering just how much sex they'd had in the last forty-eight hours. Shouldn't they be a little less frantic for each other? The last time Finn could remember having a sexual marathon like this, he was in college. He couldn't speak for Grace–and it wasn't something he particularly wanted to ask her–but he hoped this wasn't the norm for her either.

She pulled up to a Holiday Inn and they both practically fell out of the truck in their haste to get inside. "I'll grab a room, you grab the bags!" she called out, walking hurriedly toward the entrance. Finn wasn't far behind and was thankful they had stopped at a drugstore earlier and grabbed another box of condoms.

Actually, he was grateful he had thought to be optimistic when he originally packed for this trip and brought condoms to begin with. He hadn't used any of them until Grace.

That realization hit him and made him smile.

Plenty of women flirted with him over the course of his trip west, and most invited him back to their rooms, but none had interested him. His brother had made fun of him nightly and accused him of being too uptight. But now he was glad he hadn't taken the bait or simply hooked up with someone just for the sake of hooking up. He never would have imagined a runaway bride being the one to pique his interest. But from the moment they met, she managed to snag all of his attention and made him act completely out of character.

And he'd never been happier or more grateful.

Five minutes later, they were in the elevator, and he had his hands full of their luggage and couldn't touch her.

Grace had no such restraints.

The second the elevator doors closed, she was pressed up against him and kissing him senseless. He wanted to throw the bags to the ground, but there was something incredibly sexy and arousing about the way she could touch him and he couldn't touch her.

As soon as they were in the room, however, he tossed the bags aside and reached for her. Grace was right there and jumped into his arms, wrapping her legs around his waist, and after that, it was all blind, wild need. It was amazing neither of them got hurt because finesse completely went out the window.

They were against the wall before twisting, turning, and stumbling over to the bed. One minute they were dressed, the next they weren't, and Finn wasn't even sure how it happened. All he knew was Grace was naked and on top of him and it was freaking glorious. If this road trip never ended, he'd be the happiest man alive.

And that was definitely saying something.

It was fast and furious, wild and dirty.

Oh, so dirty.

Some of the things they said to each other were enough to make him blush.

But damn did those words spur them both on.

Minutes later, she was breathless beside him, and he couldn't even believe they were still on top of the made bed. The pillows had scattered onto the floor, but they'd been so frantic they didn't even take the time to turn down the bed.

"That was awesome," she said, turning and smiling at him. "Much better than watching the miles roll by, don't you think?"

"Much."

She laughed softly. "One-word answer? Not much for post-coital conversation or did we kill some brain cells?"

"Both."

That only made her laugh harder. "Awesome."

Chuckling along with her, Finn forced himself to stand up. He took one of her hands in his and pulled her to her feet.

"What? What are you doing?" she said, still laughing.

With his free hand, he pulled the bedding down and then tossed her back onto the mattress. "Scoot over." And when he was beside her, he pulled the sheet up over them. "There. Isn't this better?"

"Not adventurous, huh?"

"What does that mean?"

"It bothered you that we were on top of the blankets, right?"

"I wouldn't say bothered..."

"And yet the first thing you did was get us under them," she pointed out. "And now that I think about it, you haven't been up for trying sex anywhere else but in the bed."

"Not true," he countered. "There was the High Roller."

"That doesn't count."

His eyes went wide. "Excuse me? How does that not count? That was wildly public, hot as hell, and you had a pretty spectacular orgasm if memory serves."

"Oh, it was, believe me," she replied, snuggling next to him. "But...no one was in the pod with us, so that means it wasn't public. We were five hundred feet in the air and no one could see in, so wildly public is definitely not the way I'd describe it. And besides, that was all for me. It would have been hotter if we'd done it immediately after the orgasm."

Yeah. He'd thought of that too, but he wasn't prepared for any of it at the time. That didn't mean he wasn't adventurous–which is what he said.

"Then prove it," she challenged.

"Now?" he croaked. "Grace, I know you wouldn't know it from the way we entered this room, but...I'm exhausted. I don't know about you, but I seriously need some sleep."

Laughing, she moved further under the sheets. "I didn't mean right this minute, but...I don't know, I'm just saying you should show me some time that you have an adventurous side."

He was quiet for a moment before he relaxed a little more against the pillows. With one arm around Grace, she had her head resting on his chest, and he knew he had to ask.

And hated that he even wanted to know.

Clearing his throat mildly, he asked, "So...are you usually more...uh...adventurous? Like were you and your ex...?" Finn immediately wanted to take the question back, but he knew he couldn't, and now he'd have to deal with whatever Grace told him.

Laughter wasn't the response he expected.

Looking down at her, he asked, "What's so funny?"

She lifted her head, placing her hand on his stomach to brace herself. "Oh, my God, I can't believe we're having this conversation!"

It was on the tip of his tongue to remind her that she started it, but...

"For the record, no," she explained as her laughter died away. "Jared was not the least bit adventurous and our sex life was incredibly basic."

Basic? Was that what he was?

Shifting a little beside him, she went on. "We stopped having sex two months ago. Jared said it was so our wedding night would be better, but now I think it was because he was sleeping with Steph. I guess I should be thankful he wasn't sleeping with both of us at the same time." She shuddered. "Total ick-factor."

He nodded.

Sighing, she flopped down beside him onto her back and stared up at the ceiling. "Can I tell you something?"

It was a mild variation on their usual conversation starter and it made him smile. "Sure."

"I don't know why I was going to marry him," she said

quietly. "Looking back, I never should have accepted his proposal."

Finn wanted to ask why she did, but he didn't know how to do it without sounding accusatory.

"So many of my friends were engaged and getting married, and I thought I should too. We were compatible, and things were comfortable, but now I know that's not what marriage should be like."

Okay, now he was intrigued because he had always thought those were good qualities for a marriage. "What do you mean?" Rolling onto his side, he continued. "Being compatible is important to a relationship–and especially for a marriage. Most people find that to be the number one important component when looking to spend their life with someone."

Grace turned her head and looked at him. "No, no... you're right. It is. But there needs to be more!" Now she propped herself on her side to face him, and Finn had a fleeting thought of how it was kind of cool how they were lying here in bed, naked, and having a completely normal conversation. "There should be love and mutual respect for each other. And I'm not talking love like you'd say you love your best friend or even your family. But the kind of love that makes your heart race every time that person walks into a room!"

Her face was so animated and she sounded so passionate that Finn found himself wanting to know more.

"Marriage should be forever! No one wants to stay married anymore! You have to be able to work through your problems and compromise! God, Jared never wanted to compromise! It was his way or no way, and that's how I got roped into that damn destination wedding without my family."

Wow, he thought.

"And you know, I should have known better. I'm an intelligent woman who studies people's behavior for a lot of my job and I didn't see just how self-centered he was." She was on a roll now. "He was all about appearances and how things made *him* look. Like if we were going out, he'd want approval on my outfit so he could be sure it would look good next to him."

Yeah, Finn's original thoughts on the guy were correct–he was a douche.

"And sex?" She let out a mirthless laugh followed by a snort of disgust. "It was always about him! Foreplay was almost non-existent, and it never mattered to him if I climaxed or not. Ever! And the most adventurous place we'd ever done it was on his living room sofa and I think that was only because there was a football game on and he wanted to catch the score!"

Correction, he was a total douche.

"Grace, I...I don't even know what to say to that. And to be honest, I'm not sure I know why you told me."

She shoved him until he was on his back and then crawled on top of him–straddling him like some sort of sexy warrior. "Because this is what people do, Finn! We share things about ourselves so the person we're with understands us better."

Okay. That made sense.

"I want you to know things about me," she went on, "and I want to know things about you."

Resting his hands behind his head, he asked, "What would you like to know?"

She considered him for a moment. "Would you be opposed to sex in a shower?"

"Uh...no..."

"Would you freak out if I wanted sex in the kitchen?"

Finn looked around the room and confirmed there wasn't one in here but knew what she was implying. "As long as it wasn't a public kitchen, like the one at the IHOP or something, I'd be fine with that."

"What about the car? Would you ever have sex in a car?"

"So we're only getting to know each other where sex is concerned?"

"For now," she said lightly. "So? Sex in a car?"

"I don't think it would be particularly comfortable in our rental."

"Finn..." she whined.

He shrugged. "Lost my virginity in a car, and most of my sexual activities in high school happened that way, so no. I'm not opposed to that." And before she could ask another question, he quickly added, "However, our rental isn't particularly roomy, so I'd opt for something with a backseat if possible if that's where you were planning on going next."

She gave a curt nod. "Public places?"

"The High Roller wasn't public enough?"

Then she laughed. "We already covered that. We were alone, and it wasn't public. Let it go. I'm talking parks, golf courses, the bathroom of a JCPenney..."

"Wow, you've really given this some thought," he said with a chuckle. "Or are you naming places you've already done it?"

She shook her head. "Nope. Never in any of those places."

"Okay then," he replied, thinking about it. "Parks? Plenty of private trails and bushes to hide behind, so...sure. Golf course? I don't golf, but I wouldn't give it a hard no based on that. And the bathroom of a JCPenney? I don't shop there, but then again, I avoid the mall at all costs. Still, it could be fun. But the acoustics could totally be a distraction."

For a minute, she only stared at him unblinking, and Finn wondered if he answered correctly. Then she leaned down and gave him a fierce hug and kissed him soundly.

He guessed he did.

The next day they vowed to put a few more miles in to make up for the half-day of driving they lost in Amarillo.

Something Grace did not regret one bit.

The extra time with Finn had been everything. After their adventurous sex talk, they slept for almost five hours. They'd showered together–and it was amazing–before they went to dinner, and then spent the night sitting in bed together watching TV. They'd argued over what to watch–he wanted to watch some sort of live cop drama, and all the shows she enjoyed were on channels the hotel didn't get, so they agreed to compromise, ended on HGTV and spent the night talking about houses and home improvements.

And it was the most fun she'd ever had while watching TV.

It turns out Finn wasn't only knowledgeable about fixing cars, but he was also pretty knowledgeable about fixing houses–a quality she found ridiculously attractive. Maybe it was a cliché, but there was just something incredibly sexy about a man who worked with his hands. The entire time he talked, Grace envisioned him shirtless, in a pair of faded jeans and a tool belt.

Even thinking about it now was enough to make her drool a little.

Not while driving...not while driving...

Yeah, they had talked about not getting distracted by sexy talk while they were driving. There were miles to make up and even if she wasn't feeling particularly anxious to get home, she was respectful of the fact that Finn was. He had a life to get back to–a business.

And that had her thinking about how skilled he was. He shared with her all about the home improvements he'd done on his own place–installing hardwood floors, building a deck, and renovating his master bathroom. The more he talked, the more it became like catnip to her.

Jared didn't do anything for himself–he'd even hired someone to hang shelves for him in his apartment!

Ugh...

A lot of this was hindsight, but Grace knew she had always been attracted to guys who were...you know...rugged and worked with their hands. Unfortunately, she always dated prissy guys in suits. Why? Why did she do that?

Because I'm stupid, that's why...

She refused to let herself go there today. They had stopped briefly in Oklahoma City for lunch on their way to Memphis. It was a lot longer of a driving day than either of them originally planned, but they really did need to make up some time. If they kept up at the rate they had been going, it would be another full week before they got to Atlanta. And again, while that was more than okay with her, she knew Finn needed to get back to work. In a perfect world, they could take all the time they wanted, and they'd get to stop each day and explore the sights and enjoy the cities they stopped in.

And she really wanted to spend some time in Memphis

but didn't know how to tell Finn that. It seemed crazy for them to be near so many great tourist spots and not stop to see them! Maybe he was used to seeing them, but Grace never had, and who knew if she'd ever take the opportunity to do it again? Even though they'd talked about this exact thing and she promised to let him set the pace...it was Memphis! Actually, it had always been her dream to see Nashville, but it was totally not on the route, so she was definitely going to keep that to herself. But maybe...

Finn was driving this stretch of the trip because it was longer, and Grace was fine with that. She enjoyed driving, but she enjoyed sitting back and relaxing a bit more. The windows were down, it was a beautiful day, and she really was feeling good–at peace. If anyone had told her a road trip with a stranger was going to be the best therapy for dealing with running out on her wedding, she would have told them they were crazy. And yet...here she was, and she was thankful for the crazy circumstances that brought her here.

And to Finn.

Knowing she needed to approach this next topic carefully, she reached over and placed her hand on his thigh. He gave her a sexy grin and she actually felt a fluttering in her belly. Every time he looked at her it was like that, and she loved it.

"It's nice how there isn't a lot of traffic today, huh?"

He nodded. "Definitely. And the weather's great so really, we're gonna make good time getting to Memphis."

"Mmm...it really is a beautiful day. I almost wish this truck wasn't a truck. I wish it were a convertible. It's the perfect day to drive with the top down, right?"

Finn looked over at her. "A convertible, huh? That definitely would have been cool."

Nodding, she racked her brain for a way to broach the

subject without being too obvious. "Of course, my hair would have been a complete mess by the time we stopped later on. Some girls can pull off the windblown look. Unfortunately, I'm not one of them."

He chuckled. "Somehow, I doubt that. Your hair has looked good every day, whether it's been up in a ponytail or down and loose."

"Aww..." She squeezed his thigh. "That was very sweet of you to say."

"I only speak the truth."

Okay, it was time to pull off the bandage and just get it over with. "So...I was thinking," she began.

"You want to spend extra time in Memphis, don't you?" he said, totally stealing her thunder.

"What? How did you know?" Dammit, was she *that* predictable?

"For starters, you've asked several times about how long it would take to get to Memphis, what time you thought we'd arrive in Memphis, would I want to go and get something to eat right away when we got there or if I would be too tired to go out." He paused and grinned at her again. "At first I thought you were just making conversation or perhaps hinting how you wanted to get right to the room for a repeat of yesterday, but the Elvis playlist you started up an hour ago really sealed the deal."

"Well, drat," she pouted, crossing her arms over chest. "Done in by my own music choices."

"I realize you have a very eclectic taste in music, but one Elvis song after another really clued me in that you were trying to make a statement."

And here she was thinking she was clever. Ha!

"We're not going to get into the city until almost eight

tonight," he said. "So other than dinner, I don't think we're going to get to see or do much else."

"Oh."

"However..."

She instantly perked up, twisting in her seat to face him. "However...?"

"Our next stop after Memphis is Birmingham, Alabama, and it's a little less than four hours away so... maybe we can tour some stuff in the morning and leave after lunch. Maybe around two. What do you think? Would that work for you and give you enough time to satisfy your curiosity?"

If it weren't so dangerous, Grace would have climbed across the seat to hug him. "Really? You're not just messing with me?" she asked excitedly.

"Would I do that to you?"

She shrugged. "I don't know. You have mentioned several times how I'm a pain in the ass, so maybe..."

"Uh-uh. I never used those words. I said you drive me crazy. That's completely different."

He was adorable, she thought. And a super considerate guy. "So what I'm hearing is that you *really* want to tour Graceland too. Right? That's what I'm hearing?"

Chuckling, he shook his head. "Would there be any point in disagreeing?"

"None! And just so you know, tours start at eight in the morning, so we totally have time to do it and see a little of the city before we hit the road. Yay!" Bouncing a little in her seat, she clapped her hands and started talking about all the other things they could see and do while in Memphis.

By the time that topic had been exhausted, she almost felt as if she'd visited the city already and was ready to talk about something else.

"After Birmingham, we'll be in Atlanta, right?"

He nodded but didn't comment, and Grace realized it wasn't a topic she was particularly ready to embrace either. That meant their trip was almost over. He was going to go back to work, she was going to fly home, and then...that was it. It was a seven-hour drive from Raleigh to Atlanta and that meant seeing each other wasn't really an option. Sure, people did the long-distance relationship thing all the time, but...hell, she wasn't even sure it was something Finn would be interested in. What they were doing now was fun and exciting, and it had a time limit. For all she knew, he was looking forward to her finally going home so he could get his life back to normal. Of course, first he'd have to deal with his brother and that whole mess, but after that, he was a responsible man who had his own life to handle. Would he really want to continue to see her knowing she was a bit of a mess right now?

But wait, was she?

As cold and callous as it sounded, she really didn't have any messy feelings toward Jared. Was she angry? Yes. Did she wish hateful things on him? Absolutely! Having his penis fall off was her number one wish, but...that was never going to happen and she should just let it go. But other than that, her life with Jared was over. They hadn't moved in together, there wasn't going to be any major separating of their lives because...

Wow. They had never really been joined. Again, why hadn't she seen that before?

A weary sigh was out before she could stop it.

"You okay?" Finn asked.

"Yeah, just...thinking."

She really didn't want to talk to him about this—felt like she'd already shared *way* more than she should have about her previous relationship, and none of it made her look good. It was time to think of something else.

"What's your favorite food?" she asked, forcing all negative thoughts from her mind.

He looked at her like she was crazy but quickly returned his attention to the road. "Steak."

"Ooh...good choice. Please tell me you like it rare."

He laughed. "As if there's any other way."

"Favorite color?"

"Blue."

"Favorite band?"

"The Foo Fighters."

"Biggest fear?"

"Flying."

Right. She remembered that. "Hobbies?"

He was quiet for a moment. "Even though I work on cars for a living, it's what I enjoy doing in my spare time too. I love rebuilding engines. Besides that, I'd have to say working with wood. I told you last night about the work I did on my house and it really was incredibly fulfilling."

"Play any sports?"

"I'm on a softball team and I did play both baseball and football in high school." Then he grinned at her. "But I haven't played since."

"Biggest pet peeve?"

"People who ask too many questions," he replied, but Grace could see his lips twitching.

"Ha, ha. Very funny. Excuse me for trying to play a game to pass the time."

"I'm just glad you didn't suggest the license plate game."

"The what?"

His bark of laughter was his first response. "You don't

know what the license plate game is?" Then he explained the rules of the game to her.

"Finn, we've discussed this. I've never been on a road trip before! How would I know what that is?"

"Okay, fair enough. Got any more questions?"

Did she? Hell yes! For all the talking she and Finn had done over the last several days, Grace knew there was still so much she didn't know about him. And because their time was coming to an end, she felt like she needed to know more. "Absolutely!" she said, forcing a smile. "Favorite ice cream flavor?"

"Chocolate. Yours?"

"Chocolate, too. Isn't everyone's?"

"Probably not. Dave loves strawberry."

"Just another reason not to like him," she teased. "Um... first car?"

"A 2005 Ford Ranger. Black." He paused. "I loved that truck."

"Wow, so not much newer than this one, right?"

He nodded.

"What do you drive now?" She was certain he had told her since it was clearly the car his brother stole, but for the life of her, she couldn't remember.

"A 2018 Ford Mustang. And it better still be unharmed and in one piece when I get home," he murmured. "If Dave so much as put one scratch on that car..."

"Okay, okay, okay," she said soothingly. "I'm sure the car is going to be fine. And if not, it's a good thing you know a mechanic!" She was going for light and funny, but he didn't look amused.

"New topic—alien abductions! Friend or foe?"

They were in the right-hand lane on the interstate, and Finn pulled over onto the shoulder, put the truck in park and looked at her. "Did you bump your head or something?"

"What? No. Why?"

"Alien abductions? Friend or foe? What the hell kind of question is that? Are you having a stroke or something?"

Grace couldn't tell if he was genuinely concerned or amused. "No! I...um...I don't know. I just...it came to mind and thought it would be a good distraction from the way the conversation was going! Why is it such a big deal?"

In the blink of an eye, he reached out and banded one rough hand around her nape and pulled her in for a quick and steamy kiss. "I've said it before and I'll say it again..."

"I make you crazy," she finished for him, smiling against his lips. "Good."

Finn straightened in his seat and pulled back onto the road. "How about I pick the topic this time?"

She sighed dramatically. "Fine, but it better not be boring."

Shaking his head, he laughed. "Right. Because my favorite color was completely riveting."

"You know it."

"I think it's time to shine the spotlight on Grace for a little while," he said lightly. "See how you like it."

"Bring it, Kavanagh." She cracked her knuckles and made a big production of looking like she was preparing for battle.

"Favorite food?"

"Chinese food–anything spicy!"

"Favorite color?"

"Hot pink."

He nodded. "Favorite band?"

"Not so much a band, but an artist–Taylor Swift."

With a quick shudder, he continued. "Biggest fear?"

"Drowning." When he looked at her, she nodded. "When I was a kid, we went to the beach, I went out a little too far in the ocean and the current started to carry me. It was terrifying. I don't go in the ocean anymore past my knees. Pools, I can handle. But lakes or other bodies of water I avoid."

"Interesting. Hobbies?"

"Hmm...love to read, love to cook." When he looked at her with surprise, she laughed and nodded. "It's true! I love watching cooking shows and trying new recipes! It's so much fun! Not so much when I'm only cooking for me, but I still enjoy it."

"Do you bake?"

She shook her head. "Oh, God, no. I hate measuring."

"But...you just said you love cooking!"

"Two completely different things. It's all about precision when you're baking, and I don't have that kind of patience. I like to concoct and create and play around with ingredients. That's a fairly big no-no when you bake."

"Okay, I get it. So, any sports?"

"I'm a bit of a klutz, and I never played sports or took dance classes or anything like that when I was growing up. But now I enjoy yoga and Zumba and going to the gym and taking some classes."

He paused. "Biggest pet peeve?"

"People who avoid answering questions," she said sassily and was glad he laughed with her. "What else you got?"

"Hmm...most adventurous place you've ever had sex?"

Oh, God... "We've been PG-rated all day, Finn," she said lightly. "And I thought we agreed to no more sexy talk while one of us is driving. You sure you want to take this in the R-rated direction when we've still got hours to go before stopping for the night?"

"Well, I wasn't asking for specifics," he clarified, "just a location."

"Alright...it was under the bleachers on the football field of my high school," she said, hanging her head in embarrassment. "It was late at night–not during a game or anything, so...no chance of anyone catching us. Not really. At least...I don't think anyone could have caught us."

Lame, Grace. Totally lame.

"Mine was in a tent on a camping trip," he said, sounding casual. "There were about a dozen of us and we were going to go off into the woods, but she was afraid of getting too many mosquito bites!" Looking over at her, he grinned. "Adventurous, right?"

"Very!" she said heartily.

"Okay, want to stay R-rated or go back to PG?"

The thought of another R-rated question intrigued her. "Keep it going, Finn. Let's see what else you got."

"Sex toys? Yay or nay?"

"Ooh...yay."

He nodded in approval. "Morning sex or evening sex?"

"Love them both, but I'm finding out that morning sex is really good."

And if she wasn't mistaken, he was blushing. Totally adorable.

"Do you prefer to be on the top?"

"Ooh...another good question." She stopped and thought about it. "Depends on my mood, but there is something to be said about having a sexy man stretched out on top of me." She looked at him, lifted her sunglasses and winked. "I really like that."

"Ever had a threesome?"

"Oh, my gosh! No!"

"Good to know," he said, laughing softly. "Ever have phone sex?"

Laughing a little, she said, "No, but I always thought it could be hot."

He nodded. "Ever watch porn?"

She eyed him carefully. "A couple of times. Not really my thing, but I do enjoy a good, sexy erotic novel. It makes me use my imagination." Her voice was a little breathless and she couldn't even explain why.

"Okay. Uh...good. I mean...using your imagination is a good thing," he said gruffly. "Um...bondage, yay or nay?"

"Are we talking with silk scarves or chains? Because I wouldn't be opposed to the silk, but I might have issues with the chains."

His only response was to cough until he was almost choking. Grace gave him a moment to recover before speaking again.

"Finn?"

"Hmm?"

"I think we need to go back to the PG questions," she said, squirming in her seat.

"How come?"

"Because if we keep going with this, we're going to have to find out how to maneuver having sex in this truck, on the interstate, right now."

Laughing, he said, "So, are you a cat or a dog person?"

8

IT WAS THEIR LAST NIGHT.

Sighing, Grace looked out the window of their hotel room and wished she could stop time–not forever, but for at least another week or so. She was completely conflicted. Part of her really wanted to get home to see her family, but the rest of her selfishly wanted more time with Finn. They would need a clean break tomorrow. She was going to drop him off at his shop so he could grab a car–he had several loaners he kept on hand–and she was going to head to the airport.

At least, that was the plan, even though she hadn't booked her flight yet.

She was procrastinating, plain and simple.

Finn stepped in close behind her, his hands resting on her waist. They had chosen a more upscale hotel for the night–one that offered room service. It was the first time on this entire trip that she had zero interest in going out and exploring. All she wanted to do was stay in with Finn and soak up all she could of him.

He'd changed her.

In these few short days, Grace felt like she was a completely different person than who she was when she left for Lake Tahoe. Her eyes were opened to all the ways she wasn't taking care of herself and how she had allowed Jared to control too much of her life. That was all over and done with, and from here on out, she was focusing on the things she wanted to do. Plus, she was ready to spend some much-needed time with her family.

His arms came around her and he rested his head against hers. "Dinner will be here in thirty minutes."

She nodded. "Okay."

They stood like that–staring down at the city–for several minutes. "You know we're going to have to talk eventually, right?" he asked quietly.

"Why?" she whispered, hating the tremor in her voice. "We both know what's coming. Why do we have to talk about it again?"

Gently, he turned her in his arms until she was facing him. "I hate this, too, you know."

That surprised her. "You do?"

He nodded. "Yeah, I do."

"But...but I thought..."

"When this whole trip started, I thought we'd drive, and it would be awkward, but we'd get through it and go our separate ways. But it didn't take long for me to realize that wasn't going to happen."

"Finn..."

"It's true. Things were messy for both of us and yet...I was drawn to you. I didn't want to be because it was only going to complicate things, but I want you to know I wouldn't change a thing, Grace. Not one. I don't regret any of it."

"Me either," she said, feeling tears stinging her eyes as

she willed them away. "You know I've always been honest with you, right?"

"Almost painfully so," he teased lightly, and that made her smile.

"I'm not ready for tomorrow. I...I'm just not. Every time I think about it, it feels wrong. I hate that we live seven hours apart. I hate that I can't just...throw South Carolina out of the way so our states could be closer!"

"If anyone could do it, Grace, it would be you." He reached up and caressed her cheek.

"It's not fair. How could I find you and lose you all in the span of a week?" And then she wanted to kick herself for her admission. That was a lot more information than he probably bargained for. Resting her forehead against his chest, she said, "Tell me I'm crazy. Tell me I'm wrong and the feeling isn't mutual. Put me out of my misery."

He was quiet for so long that she was fairly certain he was just trying to find the words to let her down easy. If nothing else, Finn Kavanagh was a good guy.

Both his hands–those wonderfully rough hands– cupped her face and slowly forced her to look at him. "You're not crazy," he said, his voice so low and gruff that it almost didn't sound like him. "And you're not wrong." Pausing, he let out a long, slow breath before adding, "And the feeling is mutual. This wasn't supposed to happen."

Nodding, she quietly replied, "I know. Is it...do you think...is this just proximity? Are we just reacting to each other like this because we were forced to be together?"

"That's not even possible, Grace. I spent several days in Carson City, and I met a lot of women..."

She tried to pull away, but Finn wouldn't let her.

"And I wasn't interested in any of them. Only you." His arms dropped to wrap around her and he held her tight. "I can't explain it–any of it. And I have no idea what's going to happen after tomorrow or how we'll feel once we're back in our own homes and back to our usual routines and lives."

And dammit, she knew he was right. He was always practical and logical and saw things in a way that she couldn't because her emotions got in the way.

Tucking a finger under her chin, he gave her a sad smile. "I don't want this to be the mood tonight. We're going to have a nice dinner here in the room and then..."

She looked at him expectantly. "And then what?"

Then his smile went from sad to sexy. "And then we have sex anywhere in this room–or, out in the hotel–that you want."

Her eyes went wide. "Really?"

He nodded. "Absolutely. You want to go do it in a supply closet? I'm your guy."

"Wow!"

"You want to go down to the lobby and hit one of the bathrooms and test the acoustics? Stick with me."

"I like where this is going."

"And...I'm not making any promises, but...there is a mall less than a mile away. We can go there, and we can do it in any bathroom or dressing room you want. What do you say?"

Oh, God, she thought. This man was everything!

When she didn't respond, he lowered his head until they were cheek to cheek, and he whispered in her ear, "Or we can stay right here where I can lay you down on the bed, sprawl out on top of you, and give you more orgasms than you can handle. All. Night. Long."

Her knees buckled as his words rumbled against her skin, and he caught her, hauled her back up, and kissed her with more passion and need than Grace thought possible. It was a kiss that said a million little things and hers responded in kind. Every time Finn kissed her, it got better and better, and if this is how they spent the rest of their night, she'd be a very happy woman.

One minute his lips were devouring her, and the next she felt herself being lifted off her feet. "Finn!" she cried, clutching his shoulders. "What are you doing?"

"We have some time before the food gets here," he explained as he carried her across the room. "And I thought we'd try out the acoustics in our bathroom first." They were already in there and he placed her down on the vanity counter and whipped her shirt up and over her head. "What do you think, Grace? You wanna try it out?"

She mimicked his move by pulling his shirt off as well. "Definitely."

"Your shirt's been driving me crazy all day," he said huskily.

"Really? Why?"

"I loved the way the words 'Girl Power' stretched perfectly over your breasts. Very sexy."

That made her smile. "You're sexy."

When she leaned in to kiss him, he held her off. "I just want you to know something."

"What?"

"I know this wasn't the adventurous romp we talked about, but..."

And at that moment, she noticed the uncertainty, the vulnerability, and if she wasn't already falling for him, this would totally seal the deal. Placing a finger over his lips, she said, "I talk a good game about wanting to be a little wilder and more uninhibited, but the truth is, I don't care where we make love. As long as it's with you, it's the greatest adventure ever."

And this time, when she leaned in to kiss him, he totally let her.

The room was dark, and Grace was sleeping beside him. Finn glanced over at the clock and saw it was after two. In a perfect world, he would have taken her out for a romantic dinner in a five-star restaurant after bringing her flowers. After dinner, they would have walked around at an art gallery or maybe through a park, or maybe they would have gone dancing. Instead, what did he have to offer? Room service in a boutique hotel in Birmingham after five days on the road.

The circumstances couldn't be helped, but that didn't mean he didn't wish things were different.

How could I find you and lose you all in the span of a week?

Her words from earlier came back to him, and her honesty humbled him. She was far braver than he ever was or ever could be. All week he'd struggled with how he felt about her because who fell that hard that fast? It wasn't natural, was it? Did people really do that? And if they did, did it last?

And that was his biggest fear.

It was all fine and well to think you were falling for someone at first sight, but where were you a month later? Six months later? A year later?

A lifetime later?

Yeah, he went there. How could he not? Over the last five days, he and Grace had spent more time together—more hours sitting and talking and getting to know each other—than most couples did in their first month or two of dating.

When Finn said he wanted to cram as much as possible into their time together, he believed they really did. From her crazy interview questions to listening and watching her reactions to all the places they visited and explored, he knew in his heart that he knew this woman better than he'd ever known any other woman in his life.

Morning would be here before they knew it, and the drive to Atlanta was relatively short. They could realistically be at his shop by lunchtime. Grace could be back in Raleigh by dinner.

With her family.

Without him.

How was it possible that even just *thinking* about not sharing a meal with her filled him with despair?

He needed to get a grip. Tomorrow they would say goodbye, but it wasn't going to be forever. It couldn't be. Yes, she had to go back home and back to her job and so did he. This was the longest he'd ever been away from the shop and he was already fairly certain he was going to be putting in long hours for the next week. As for Grace, he had no idea what her work schedule was going to be like, but considering she was coming home after a canceled wedding, he was pretty sure her time was going to be filled with visits from family and friends who wanted to comfort her.

I want to comfort her.

And the thing was, Finn knew he had. If anything, he had tried to be a friend to her this week and listened when she needed to talk and held her when she needed to cry. He'd like to think he helped, but he wasn't completely clueless. He knew there was nothing like the comfort of your family when things were wrong. He only hoped she didn't feel bad for long.

Then his mind wandered to his own crappy situation.

His time with Grace had been an amazing distraction, and it certainly helped him lose some of his rage, but...it couldn't be ignored forever. No amount of time surrounded by his friends and family was going to change the fact that his brother had done something unforgivable.

However...if it hadn't been for Dave stealing his car, he never would have met Grace.

Now he was torn. How mad could he *really* be? If he let it go and just grabbed his keys from his brother and said no harm done, it was no different from all the other times Dave had screwed up and everyone fixed it for him. And if he did that, where would it end? What would stop his brother from pulling a stupid stunt like this again? Where was the justice? Where was the lesson?

Why is it up to me to teach him one?

There were no answers–not right now, at least.

Right now, he needed to sleep. Grace had worn him out again and there wasn't a doubt in his mind that he was going to make love to her at least one more time before they left the hotel in the morning. So yeah, he needed at least a couple of hours of sleep before he could do that.

Hugging her close, he kissed the top of her head and relaxed. The smell of her strawberry shampoo surrounded him–soothed him. As soon as his eyes closed, he was out like a light.

The next time he opened them, the room was still dark, but Grace wasn't beside him. It took a minute for his eyes to adjust to the darkness, but when they did, he saw her and his heart squeezed a little hard in his chest. She was sitting up, hugging her knees. Gently, he placed a hand on her back. "Hey," he said sleepily. "You okay?"

She shook her head. "I couldn't sleep."

Slowly, he sat up. It would be foolish to ask why. He

had no doubt that her mind was probably racing with a ton of different thoughts and scenarios of how the day was going to unfold. Glancing over at the bedside clock, Finn saw it was a little after five. His hand skimmed up her spine and then he carefully guided her back against the pillows. "Wanna talk?"

"I don't think it will do any good," she said quietly. "All the talking in the world isn't going to change anything." She curled up next to him as she always did, her head on his shoulder, her hand on his chest. "And the thing is, I know it's going to be okay. I'm not against going home. Any of the things I have to deal with because of the wedding won't be a problem–they may be a little awkward, and I'm sure I'm going to get tired of talking about it real fast–but none of it is causing me stress or anxiety."

"Okay."

"And the reality is that I would be getting back from my honeymoon in another two days and I'll have to go back to work, so...that's not going to be a problem either."

Silently, he nodded.

"Why am I overreacting like this? I mean...it's been five days! Five! Why can't I look at this like a fun time and just leave it at that?"

It was a question Finn had asked himself too, but unfortunately, he didn't have the answer either.

Grace lifted her head, and as his eyes continued to adjust to the darkness, he could see the small pout on her face. "Damn you, Finn Kavanagh," she said, but there wasn't any heat behind her words. "Why did you have to make this such a great week?"

The last thing either of them needed was for him to get all philosophical and serious. He could talk for an hour about all the reasons why they both needed the week as an escape from their lives–how they had possibly used each other as a crutch for not dealing with their different crises. Hell, if given a few minutes, he could probably find some sort of statistics on how people use sex as an emotional release and how it doesn't have to mean anything beyond the physical act.

But he wasn't going to do that.

He couldn't do that.

Mainly because he didn't believe it for a minute. They had a connection that went beyond just two people being thrown together at possibly the lowest moments in their lives. Okay, maybe he wasn't particularly at his lowest, but he was in a pretty low place. And dammit, he was done thinking about it–focusing on it. Right now, at this moment, it was about the two of them, and he pushed his old ways aside and tossed all the need to lecture out the window. If anything, someone had to lighten the mood. Normally, that was Grace's thing. But right now, he knew he needed to be the one to do it.

"Because that's my superpower," he said lightly. "Didn't you know? I'm like a little ray of sunshine swooping down to rescue damsels in distress."

She laughed softly and lay back down. "You're a jerk."

"Says you and my brother."

"Ugh...I'm sorry."

"For what?"

"You're really going to have to deal with him later on today, aren't you?"

"Yup."

"That's why I'm sorry. Here I am worrying about me and you've got some pretty serious stuff to deal with yourself. Any idea what you're going to do or say?"

"Not a clue. I keep waffling between strangling him and hugging him."

And she was leaning up again. "*Hugging him*? Why?" She paused and then said, "Oh...I get it. Is that the option if your car has been returned without a scratch on it?"

Finn shook his head. "No. That option is because if it hadn't been for him pulling that jackass stunt, we wouldn't be here right now." Reaching out, he raked a hand up into her hair. "And even though right now all we keep seeing is the negative, I wouldn't trade this week with you for anything, Grace. I want you to know that."

"I feel the same way." She rested her forehead against his and sighed.

"We're going to be fine. You're going to be relieved to not be in that old truck anymore and have the freedom to dance like a Rockette if you want without listening to me complain about you nearly poking my eye out with an elbow."

"You haven't been that bad."

"But...you really did come close to blinding me a time or two."

"And I apologized."

"Still, you may want to use a little less...enthusiasm when there's someone else in the front seat. I'm just saying."

"You're really not helping here, Finn."

"Okay, okay. You're right." He paused and thought for a minute. "I'm sure you'll be more than happy to have all your own clothes back when you get home."

"Maybe."

"*And*," he went on, "you're going to be very happy to sleep in your own bed. I don't know about you, but in that one respect, there really is no place like home. I never sleep as well in a strange bed as I do in my own."

She nodded. "Yeah, I'm the same. This one isn't so bad, though. And the one in Vegas was pretty good too."

He was about to say that any bed he shared with her was amazing, but what good would that do? He was trying to make her feel better, not worse. And reminding her of things like that could only make her sad.

So he stayed quiet.

"And I'm sure you're going to enjoy not listening to any more of my crazy playlists," she said with a hint of humor.

"I'll miss the *High School Musical* soundtrack the most," he teased, and they both laughed.

"Just so you know, you did really great learning the choreography to '*We're All in This Together*.' You should be proud."

He chuckled again. "I can't wait to show all the guys in the shop."

"Ugh…" she groaned, flopping back down beside him. "You're going to go back to work, tell everyone what a dork I am and how awful it was to get stuck with me and then forget all about me. I know it. And really, I don't blame you. I dragged you to some ridiculous places, made you arrive home two days late, and, overall, was a hot mess. I bet you're already thinking, 'Good riddance,' right?"

To the average person, Grace was just talking out loud and saying things to make herself feel better. But Finn had learned a lot over the last week and he heard the vulnerability in her voice. Turning onto his side, he smiled down at her. "Watching the beer-drinking goats was kind of interesting and not something I even knew existed."

"Don't forget the flea circus," she reminded him.

"How could I forget?" He scratched himself dramatically for effect.

"Oh, stop!" But he noticed she scratched a little herself.

"Grace Mackie, I want you to know something."

"What?"

"You didn't drag me anywhere," he explained softly but firmly. "If I didn't want to stop or didn't want to go some-place, I would have not only said something, but I wouldn't have gone. All the things you talked me into doing helped me."

"They did?"

He nodded. "Yeah, they did. I tend to take myself a little too seriously—something my brother and pretty much anyone who knows me will tell you. But you helped me break away from that pattern this week, and to that, I say thank you."

"Oh, Finn..."

"It's true. And I'm sure I'll go right back into worka-holic, control-freak mode once I'm back at the shop, but that doesn't mean I regret any of the things we did or that I will ever forget you. Because I won't."

She was quiet for so long Finn thought she had fallen asleep, but he heard her soft sniffle and knew she hadn't.

"Finn?"

"Hmm?"

"We need to make this a clean break, right?"

It pained him to agree because his heart told him it wasn't what he wanted, but the logical side of him knew it was for the best. "A clean break."

As if of one mind, they rolled toward each other and embraced. Kissing the top of her head, he said, "Let's try to get some sleep, okay?"

Grace was one step ahead of him, yawning broadly. "Okay."

Maybe their little conversation gave her some peace, maybe it didn't. All Finn knew was that all the words in the world weren't going to stop the passage of time. They were going to get up in a few hours and drive the last leg of their trip. Grace was going to go her way and he was going to go his. Was it going to be sad? Yes. Did he wish it could be different? Yes. Was there anything he could do to change it?

He yawned and hugged her close.

No.

It was a gray and dreary day.

The drive was uneventful.

All morning she had done her best to present an image of being totally calm and cool and collected. Even her t-shirt said, "Stay Cool," and had a picture of Snoopy wearing sunglasses. And all morning she had to work at channeling her inner Snoopy to keep her emotions in check.

So far, so good.

Then again, nothing out of the ordinary had happened.

Pulling up to Finn's garage was almost anticlimactic.

They had talked and decided that Grace would leave for the airport after dropping him off. They weren't going to have lunch together, and they weren't going to have a long goodbye. He wanted her to simply let him out and head to the airport.

"Son of a bitch!"

She looked over at him and saw him angrily climbing from the truck, slamming the door behind him. It didn't take long for her to see what had grabbed his attention and why.

His car was here.

At least...she thought it was his car. It was a new Mustang, but...it didn't look good.

Hesitantly, she got out and followed him. The last time

she had seen him this angry, they were in Vegas confronting his brother.

Finn was circling the car while muttering curses. He raked his hands through his hair and pulled. She could see the veins in his neck bulging as his face got redder and redder. As much as she hated to admit it, it was kind of a good thing Dave wasn't here. Otherwise...

"Well, well, well, look who *finally* decided to come back!"

Oh, Dave, she thought. *You stupid, stupid man.*

And it looked like there was about to be a big confrontation.

Turning, Grace spotted Dave walking across the parking lot, and he didn't look the least bit remorseful. If anything, he had a bit of a swagger to him–a cockiness that he really shouldn't own. She studied him and realized he looked a lot like Finn. Not as tall or as handsome, but there were enough similarities that you knew they were brothers. Looking at him, she almost felt sorry for him. It must be hard to the be the younger, less attractive, and clearly less talented brother to someone like Finn. But still, it didn't give him a free pass to be a jackass all the time.

"I'm talking to you, big brother!" Dave taunted. "That car of yours is a piece of crap!"

Groaning, she hung her head and shook it. *This isn't going to end well.*

"What the hell did you do, Dave?" Finn yelled, motioning to the car. "How could you do this?"

"If you hadn't gotten the cops after me, none of this would have happened!" Dave replied loudly. "Lucky for you I was able to outrun them and get away before they took the car and impounded it or something!" They were almost toe to toe now and Dave leaned in obnoxiously close and said, "You're welcome."

Oh, no, he didn't...

"Are you seriously expecting me to thank you?" Finn cried. "For *stealing* my car? Causing God knows how much damage? And my car is not a piece of crap!"

A snort of disgust was his brother's first response. "Oh, really? Then answer me this–how come it wasn't sturdier? I mean, look at it!" Dave took a step back and nodded and then looked over at Grace. He gave her a knowing smirk. "Seems to me it all worked out well for you, so...yeah. If anything, I got the short end of the stick! And what the hell was up with canceling the credit card? I had to sleep in the damn car, thanks to you!"

Finn sputtered and seemed to try to say at least a dozen things at once, but none of them were being articulated particularly well. She knew he was angry and frustrated, but he wasn't the least bit intimidating to his brother. If anything, Dave looked extremely amused.

"So look," Dave said, still smirking. "You're going to need a new front tire–should probably just replace all of them–and the front passenger quarter panel is pretty messed up so you'll need to take it to a body shop. And the passenger side mirror is gone." He chuckled. "I don't even know when that happened!"

Grace noticed how Finn's hands were clenching into fists and then releasing as he listened to his brother talk. She wondered why he wasn't grabbing him and shaking him. If it were her, she would have punched him in the throat by now.

"You're paying for all of this, Dave," Finn said firmly.

"What? Why?"

Grace had to bite her own tongue to keep from responding.

"*Why?* Because you *did* this!" Finn snapped. "The car was in pristine condition when we were in Carson City! This is going to be a couple thousand dollars to repair everything!"

"And where am I supposed to get the money for that?" Dave demanded. "Didn't you just hear me say how I had to sleep in the car? If I had a couple of grand lying around, I wouldn't have had to do that!"

"That really isn't my problem! And what happened to all your Vegas winnings?"

Taking a small step back, Dave scrubbed a hand against the back of his neck. "Uh, yeah, well...I sort of hit a couple of the smaller casinos on the way home, and...you know...my luck wasn't as good."

Finn groaned and then completely seemed to snap. "This is what I've been talking about! Everything I tried to get through to you on our trip! You don't think at all, do you? You just go and do whatever it is you want without even *considering* the consequences!"

"*Consequences?* I thought I'd double my money and then I could have a little breathing room so you'd get off my back! It's not my fault these smaller casinos have shifty dealers! I was ahead by almost a grand when..."

"Do you even hear yourself?" Finn yelled. "It's not the dealers' fault, it's yours! How can you not get that?"

Seemingly ignoring Finn's question, Dave continued with his own train of thought. "I was up by almost a grand when I started to lose! With all the shit with the damage to the car, I figured if I won enough, I would be able to get it fixed! But that all fell through! I couldn't get my groove back, and eventually, I got thrown out of the last casino!"

"Dammit, Dave!"

"Yeah, yeah, yeah...go ahead! Lecture me! Tell me more about what a screwup I am! You know you're dying to!" Then he glanced over at Grace and frowned. "I'm sure you've been having a field day playing the sympathy card with this one. And I'm sure you've been filling this bimbo's head with just how awful I am and how you're going to beat the crap out of me when you get home! So, bring it on! Show off for the tart!"

Grace knew Finn was at his limit, saw his fists were now completely clenched, but...so was she.

"You son of a bitch!" she cried, storming over and wind-mill kicking him in the face. Dave stumbled back with a howl of pain right before Finn's fist connected with his jaw.

"*Tart?*" she yelled at Dave, who was rolling around on the ground. "Where do you get off calling *me* a tart? And for that matter, how old are you? A hundred? No one even uses that word anymore!"

"What the hell!" Dave cried. "I think you broke my nose!"

"Good! And I hope Finn broke your jaw too!" Finn gently clasped her shoulder and tried to move her, but she had a lot of restless energy and couldn't stand still. "What an ass!"

"Okay, okay, killer. You need to calm down." He turned her to face him, and she was surprised to see him smirking. "Seriously, what was that?"

"What was what?"

"That kick! Where the hell did that even come from?"

"Oh," she began with a small laugh. "Well...remember when I mentioned how I like to take classes at the gym?"

He nodded.

"Yeah, well...I've taken a lot of martial arts classes.

Like...a lot." Winking at him, she added, "And I look super cute in my uniform."

He laughed softly. "Of course you do."

"And I do kickboxing too, so..." She shrugged. "And I took some self-defense courses too. Although this is the first time I got to use it in real life, so...yay me!" She did a happy little clap because she felt empowered.

Hugging her close, he said, "You probably shouldn't be quite so giddy about breaking someone's nose." They both looked over at Dave who was just starting to sit up.

"He totally deserved it!" she said with just a hint of defense. "He stole your car and your credit card, Finn! He left you stranded on the other side of the country! And look at your car! I'd say he deserves a heck of a lot more than a kick to the face! And on top of that, he called me a tart! *A tart!* Seriously, in my entire life, no one has ever called me a tart!"

Dave groaned, and Grace took a menacing move toward him and was glad when he flinched.

Before she could go on, Finn hauled her even closer and covered her lips with his–effectively silencing her. When he lifted his head, he wasn't smiling or smirking. If anything, his gaze was incredibly serious. "Best tasting tart I ever had."

And then they both burst out laughing.

"So glad everyone's having such a great time while I need to go to the emergency room," Dave said sarcastically as he came to his feet. He pinched the bridge of his nose, and she could tell he was silently counting to ten before commenting. Letting out a long breath, Dave looked sternly between the two of them. "You cannot just go around... kicking people in the face."

Cocking her hip, she looked at him and felt mildly

annoyed that he was basically reprimanding her after everything he'd done. "Oh, really? And you think you can just go around stealing people's cars and credit cards? How is that okay in your mind?"

"Well..."

"And, how dare you!" she interrupted, ready to fully unload on him again. "Don't go twisting this around like I'm the one who did something wrong here! This is about *you*, you loser!" she cried, shaking a finger at Dave.

"Hey!" Dave whined, still holding his nose. "Cheap shot."

"Shut up!" Finn and Grace both yelled at him.

This was not the way she envisioned her afternoon going. All morning, she imagined she'd drop Finn off, and then she'd talk him into going to lunch–even though they already said they wouldn't. Then, maybe, she'd ask to see his house. And then maybe, just maybe, she'd find a way to stay one more night. It was nothing more than a delay tactic and she knew it, but...it was what she wanted. It didn't matter that they agreed on a clean break; she wanted more time, dammit!

"C'mon, guys! I'm bleeding to death here!"

Grace looked over at Finn and saw the resignation in his face and knew...it was time. There wasn't going to be any lunch, or a house tour, or even one more night.

"You should go," Finn said quietly. "This isn't your fight, Grace. And I really should get Dave to the hospital."

"Maybe I should go with you," she blurted out. But Finn saw the suggestion for what it was.

Another delay tactic.

Shaking his head, he reached up and caressed her cheek. "No. It's time." He paused. "Clean break, remember?"

Don't cry. Don't cry. Don't cry.

"I know it's what we said," she replied with a slight tremor in her voice. "But if I *did* break his nose, then I should be the one to take care of the hospital bill." It was a legit reason even though everything in her screamed to make Dave pay for it himself for being such a jerk. One lone tear trailed down her cheek before Finn's thumb gently brushed it away. Her breath caught and she wanted to just lean into him, hold him, and not let go.

"Grace." That was all he said–just her name. But she knew what it meant.

With a curt nod, she took a step back.

And then another.

Turning, she forced herself to walk across the parking lot to the truck. Reaching behind the seat, she went to reach for Finn's bag, but suddenly he was right there beside her doing it for himself.

It was time for her to go.

This week was nothing more than a detour from her normal life, and as much as she appreciated the time away and the distraction, it wasn't real.

At least, that's what she tried to tell herself.

And it just made her incredibly sad.

They had said everything they had to say last night, and right now, they both had to get their lives back on track individually. No more leaning on each other. No more distractions.

No more...them.

There was a part of her that was waiting for Finn to stop her–for him to tell her not to go. But he didn't. If anything, he looked just as sad as Grace knew she did. They walked around to the driver's side and he opened the door for her.

"Finn, I..." but the words died in her throat when her gaze met his.

Yeah, it was time for her to go.

Sitting behind the wheel, she fastened her seatbelt as Finn closed the door. She quickly rolled down the window. He rested his hands on the door as he crouched down slightly to look at her. "Clean break." And she had to wonder if he was saying that for her or for him. "Have a good flight home, Grace. Be happy."

Seriously? That was it?

"Finn, I..."

His hands gently tapped the door as he straightened. "Don't drive the flight attendants crazy, okay?"

And then he turned and walked away, leaving Grace wondering how it was possible for her heart to hurt more right now watching Finn walk away than it had a week ago when she walked away from her own wedding.

9

It was after eight on a Friday night and Finn was bent over the engine of a 2015 Dodge Ram. He was tired and his entire body ached from the long hours he was putting in, but he didn't have anything else to do. So here he was. Everyone had gone home for the day and he kind of enjoyed having the garage to himself. In the background, he had some Florida Georgia Line playing, and he did his best to convince himself all was well.

This was just a routine tune-up he was doing, and there wasn't any reason for him to be doing it this late on a Friday night, but it was a good distraction. If he kept himself busy enough, Finn knew he wouldn't have time to think about all the ways his life was a complete shitshow and how much he'd screwed up. Hell, almost every time he closed his eyes he could still see the look on Grace's face when he wished her a safe flight. What on earth was he thinking?

Clean break.

Yeah, that was the plan, but more than anything, he had been trying not to make waves. That was always the way he'd been. When things got tough, he was the peacemaker who hated confrontation of any kind. And even though he knew that didn't quite describe their situation, he was simply trying to hold it together and do the right thing.

Like an idiot.

Still, at the time–at that moment–it was for the best. She really did need to get back to her life in North Carolina and deal with the aftermath of canceling her wedding, and he had to deal with Dave–unfortunately. And as much as he had wanted to take her up on her offer to stay, it was just prolonging the inevitable. Their lives were in different places–literally and figuratively–and until they worked on the things that initially brought them together...well...you could only hide from reality for so long.

The only positive aspect of her leaving was the fact that Dave was safer. She definitely would have kicked his brother in the face again. Or worse.

And he would have totally approved.

Stepping back from the truck, he stretched. There was nothing more he needed to do tonight. His concentration was shit and it was okay to admit he was done. The first order of business was getting something to drink. Then he needed some dinner.

"Did I even eat lunch?" he asked himself, trying to figure out where the day went. His stomach was growling, and now that he thought about it, the last thing he had was a bagel and a cup of coffee at seven this morning.

Walking into the break room, Finn grabbed a bottle of water from the refrigerator and gulped the entire thing down until he got brain freeze. Cursing, he tossed the bottle in the trash and frantically rubbed his forehead before going to wash up.

Off in the distance, he heard someone knocking on the

glass door by the reception area. His first thought was that it was Grace coming back to surprise him, but he instantly pushed it aside because he gave her no reason to come back and see him. It had been three weeks and as stubborn as he knew she could be, it bothered him how her stubbornness didn't extend to fighting for him.

Sighing, he quickly dried his hands and walked out to the reception area where he came up short.

Dave.

Son of a bitch.

Yeah, things had not gone well for Finn and his brother after Grace left. As usual, Dave played the victim and tried to make Finn the bad guy, and when that got him nowhere, he got angry and verbally abusive—also typical. But the icing on the cake was when Finn got home from their trip to the ER and received a call from his father, begging Finn to go easy on Dave.

Talk about the straw that broke the camel's back...

That led to an argument between Finn and his father, followed by one between him and his mother. They both begged him to cut his brother some slack and then made excuses for Dave. But what had really done it for him was how neither seemed too concerned about all the ways Dave had done him wrong or how his actions had cost him so much.

Finn hadn't spoken to any of them since.

The scorecard in his head was pretty much full of people *not* talking to him, and the common denominator for all those problems was standing at his door holding up a bag of takeout.

"Shit," he muttered, slowly making his way to the door. He unlocked it but didn't move to let Dave in. No matter how hungry he was or how good the food smelled, he had to stand his ground. "What do you want, Dave?"

Looking somewhat contrite for a change, Dave held up the bag which Finn now realized was from his favorite pub in town. "I saw the light on a little while ago and figured I'd find you here. I brought a peace offering–two barbecue bacon cheeseburgers and an order of crinkle fries. Can we talk?"

Everything in Finn wanted to say no–to tell Dave to go to hell and slam the door in his face–but...he didn't.

And he was blaming it on being delirious from hunger.

Stepping aside, he motioned for him to come in and then locked the door behind them. "C'mon. We can sit in the break room." And surprisingly, Dave waited for Finn to lead the way. Once they were there, Dave set the food out on the table and had a seat. Pulling out a chair, Finn sat and reached for a burger. "How's your face?"

Okay, not the most eloquent way to ask how someone was doing, but again, he was blaming his surly mood on hunger.

Dave shrugged. "Everything still kind of hurts, but...it's healing."

"Nothing was broken," Finn reminded him a little sharply. "I would have thought any pain would be gone by now."

"Me too, but...I don't know. I guess I'm a slow healer."

Or just a colossal baby, he thought darkly.

"So what's up?" he finally asked, although his focus was more on the food he was about to eat than anything else. For a long minute, there was no response, and Finn could see his brother was carefully considering his words and braced himself for whatever BS he was about to be handed.

"I'm sorry I stole your car."

Say what now?

The burger was midway to his mouth when Finn froze. "Uh...what?"

"I'm sorry I stole your car," he repeated. "And your credit card." He let out a long breath and shook his head. "I...I was completely out of line, and at the time, I thought it would be funny, but...I didn't take into consideration what I was actually doing to you." Raking a hand through his hair, he leaned back in his chair. "I'm going to pay you back for all of it. I worked out a payment plan so...you know...it won't be all at once, but you will get it all. Every dime. And just so you know, I talked to Jack over at the body shop and he told me how much the repairs cost so all the numbers I came up with are based on that and the credit card charges."

Finn shook his head and murmured, "I must be hungrier than I thought and I'm hallucinating." Without looking at Dave, he took a bite of his burger, groaning at how good it tasted.

"You're not hallucinating and I'm glad I bought the extra burger," Dave said, sliding another foil-wrapped burger toward Finn. "Here's the thing. You have no idea how hard it is to be your brother."

Tossing his burger down, Finn snorted with disgust. "I knew it! I *knew* this was somehow going to be my fault!" Standing, he kicked his chair out from behind him. "Why can't you–just for once–take responsibility for your actions?"

"I am! I am!" Dave cried, holding out his hands in surrender. "That's what I'm trying to do! I just...if you'd just let me finish, Finn, I can explain!"

"Fine. Whatever," he grumbled, grabbing his chair and sitting back down. He reached for his burger and figured if nothing else, he got a free dinner for this round of aggravation. "Go on."

Dave's sigh of annoyance was the only response, but when Finn glared at him, he continued. "I'm not proud of my behavior, okay? We drove all that way to Carson City, and we had a lot of fun, but...dammit, man, you just kept riding my ass about every little thing about my life." When Finn went to interrupt, Dave held up his hand to stop him. "And it pissed me off because you were right!"

"Excuse me?"

"Yeah, happy now?" he asked snidely and then immediately apologized. "No one likes being confronted with the unflattering truth about their lives, Finn. This can't be news to you."

Rather than say anything, he simply shrugged and took another bite of his burger.

"Believe me, if I could go back and change what I did, I would. We both know that's not possible. It was incredibly mean and immature and...I'm really sorry. You may not believe me, but it's the truth." He paused. "But here's the thing–you really did me a favor."

Finn stopped mid-chew and looked at Dave in surprise. "How?"

"By calling me out on all my bullshit. When you got back, and your girlfriend kicked me in the face..."

"She's not my girlfriend," Finn said defensively.

"We'll get to that in a minute," Dave murmured. "Here's the thing, all the times we've fought with each other, I knew exactly how you were going to react. Like, I knew when you caught up with me in Vegas, you were going to try to reason with me before you got really angry and started to yell. That's the way you do things. And I know if those security guards hadn't gotten called away, you all would have escorted me up to my room…"

"That you paid for with my card!"

Again, Dave held up a hand to stop him. "You would have escorted me up to my room and taken the keys, and I still would have been able to talk you into forgiving me and driving home with me." He paused and shook his head. "Probably could have gotten you to give me gambling money at some point too."

"Yeah, great. I'm a sucker. Great talk, Dave," Finn said sarcastically. Finishing his burger, he reached for the other even as he felt a little self-loathing at what a pushover he clearly was. Next, he dumped out the container of fries and stuffed a few of them in his mouth so he couldn't comment.

"When I left the Park MGM, I had no idea what to do! It wasn't supposed to go like that! I purposely stayed in Vegas because I knew you'd find me there! Hell, it's what I had baited you with the night before."

Shrugging, he took a bite of his burger.

"Anyway, when I got back home, I figured you'd be right behind me." Then he paused and studied Finn. "I was looking over my shoulder for the entire trip expecting to see you driving up behind me at any minute. You're a stickler for schedules, and even with a couple of casino detours, I figured we'd get here at the same time or that you might even get home first. What took you so long?"

I wanted as much time as possible with an incredibly difficult blonde who turned my life upside down…

Yeah. There was no way he was going to say that.

Without looking up, he said, "It just worked out that way. You must have been speeding."

Dave chuckled. "No doubt, but still…I really expected you home sooner."

"Sorry I ruined your plans," he deadpanned.

"So here I was, waiting for you, and then I had to wait a couple of extra days, and I got worried–like what if something happened to you? Then it would totally be my fault, and I started to panic. I felt so guilty and shitty and tried to figure out how I would possibly explain to

Mom and Dad what I did." He shook his head. "Then I went the other direction–to try to make myself feel better– and figured you were just trying to mess with me. And when you pulled up finally with your girlfriend?"

"I told you, Grace is *not* my girlfriend!"

"Yeah, yeah, yeah...whatever. When you pulled up and you just...I don't know...you came out yelling and it put me on the defensive for some reason. I swear it wasn't how I planned on things going! I taunted you because I wanted you to let me have it like you always do. I was almost desperate for you to do it! And then Grace kicked me in the face and..." He paused and looked at Finn, shaking his head again. "Dude, you really blew that. Big time."

"Excuse me?"

"Grace? Yeah, you totally blew that."

Finn put the burger down and got up to grab another bottle of water from the refrigerator. "You don't know what you're talking about."

"I disagree," Dave said mildly.

Turning, he faced his brother and fought the urge to shake him. "There was nothing to blow there, Dave. Grace and I..." He growled in frustration. "You don't know what you're talking about!" It was a lame comeback, but it was all he had.

"I'm talking about the fact that you are clearly into her! I have never seen you like that with a woman–and that's including what's-her-face who you dated all those years and then never married. Sure, the two of you were affectionate and all, but I can't ever remember you looking so damn...I don't know...smitten before. I mean...I know it wasn't the best timing, and for a little while there I was seeing double, but still."

"Yeah, you were seeing things," Finn said, hating how surly he sounded.

"Oh, please. Don't even try that. You were into her, and you're a moron for letting her leave."

"Dave, just...shut up." Normally, that was enough to get his brother to change the subject.

Not tonight.

"At any other time, I would be thinking good riddance. After all, who wants a chick who can kick like that?" He gingerly touched his nose and then let out a low laugh. "Jeez...I screw up everything and even I know you should have stopped her. You don't let a girl like her get away."

Sitting back down, Finn took a long drink before replying. "You just said having a chick who can kick like that was a bad thing, and then you say not to let one like her get away! Which is it, Dave?" But he didn't wait for a response. "Grace had a flight to catch. She was always going to leave. We said it was going to be a clean break." He wanted to take the words back as soon as he said them. What happened between them was no one else's business–least of all his brother's. Talking about her out loud like this hurt too damn much. One look at his brother, however, and he knew it would be pointless to play dumb. "Besides, having to deal with you and getting you to the emergency room was just delaying the inevitable."

"You sure about that?"

Nodding, Finn picked up the last bit of his burger. "Positive."

Dave leaned back, crossing his arms across his chest and gave a casual shrug. "She said she didn't have a flight at that point. She planned to hang out here in Atlanta for the night, but..." He shrugged.

Tossing his food back down, Finn leaned in menacingly. "What the hell are you talking about? When did you even talk to Grace?"

"The day after she left, she called to make sure I was okay." He shrugged. "She offered to pay for my visit to the ER again."

Unbelievable, he thought, leaning back in his seat irritably. "And let me guess, you let her."

But surprisingly, Dave shook his head. "Nope. I told her it wasn't necessary, and my nose wasn't broken. She argued how I should go for a second opinion because she's a fierce kicker and her kick should have broken my nose, but I assured her I was fine." Then he chuckled. "I think she was more than a little offended that she didn't cause more damage."

Finn had to hold in a laugh. Leave it to Grace to argue about something like that. Then he remembered what Dave had said. "And what do you mean she didn't have a flight? She told me she did!"

Another shrug. "Dude, don't ask me. I guess she lied to you."

And for some reason, that really bothered him. Why would she lie?

She planned to hang out here in Atlanta for the night...

"Anyway, she seemed pretty upset about the way things went down, but I got the impression it had more to do with you than the shoe-to-the-face thing," Dave went on, oblivious to the fact that Finn felt like he was going to be sick. "If

I had to take a guess, I'd say she was hoping you'd ask her to stay a little longer."

They had talked about her leaving after dropping him off. A clean break. No long goodbyes. At the time, he thought it was for the best.

Just add it to the list of all the other things you've been wrong about...

"I can ask her about it when I talk to her tomorrow, if you want," Dave said with a small smirk.

"Tomorrow?" Finn asked incredulously. Seriously, what was going on here? "Why are you talking to Grace tomorrow? Or for that matter, why are you still talking to her at all?"

Straightening, Dave stood and walked over to get himself a bottle of water. "Did you know that Grace is a career counselor?"

Finn nodded.

"Yeah, well, we got to talking after we cleared up the kick thing, and she gave me some advice on finding a job and...I don't know...she really got me thinking."

This he had to hear. For *years*, Finn and his parents had been giving Dave career advice and nothing clicked. One phone conversation with Grace and suddenly his brother had some direction? Doubtful.

"About what?" he asked, trying hard to tone down the sarcasm.

"For starters, she really helped me see that I have to stop comparing myself to you." He nodded at Finn's startled expression. "My whole life, everyone's always compared us—you were the measuring stick for everything! I kept thinking I had to do the things you did and like the things you like, but Grace helped me see how that way of thinking was doing more harm than good."

Seriously?

"So I did this online test thing–Grace sent it to me–and tomorrow we're going to go over the results and figure out what I need to do or where I need to go to get started. Isn't that great?"

Finn didn't think, he just reacted. "Do you even hear yourself? Come on, Dave! It's not possible for you to do this complete turnaround in three weeks after one conversation with Grace! It's not! We've all been trying to help you for years!"

"No, you haven't," Dave replied calmly, sitting back down. "You and Mom and Dad have been *telling* me what I'm supposed to do. Grace is the first person to talk to me like an adult and ask me what it is that *I* want to do." He took a sip of water. "I'm telling you, she's really good."

Raking a hand through his hair in frustration, Finn groaned. "To accomplish in one conversation what we've been trying to do for ten years, yeah. She must be good."

"It wasn't one conversation. We've talked about five times. And you should too. Talk to her, I mean. I think she'd like that."

His heart began to race, and suddenly he couldn't think about his brother's problems; he needed to know more about Grace. "Why? Has she asked about me?"

Dave laughed softly. "Not really, not directly, but she does mention you a lot. Like seriously, a lot. I figured if you made that much of an impression on her after only five days, maybe she's interested in you too. Now, sitting here watching your face as we talk about her, I know for sure you're into her. That day in the parking lot, I thought something was there. But now?" He nodded and his smile grew. "Why not put both of you out of your misery and call her?"

Good question.

Or maybe he was afraid to find out it really had just been a proximity thing and he was the only one with lingering feelings. He wasn't sure he'd be able to handle it if that were the case.

"She could have called me, you know. For all the times the two of you have talked, she could have just as easily made one call to me to see how I was doing or to let me know she was all right."

Dave stood again and clapped a hand on Finn's shoulder. "Brother, after the colossal way you screwed up, trust me. You need to be the one to make the call."

"What do you think of this?"

Grace looked up from her computer and found her mother standing in the doorway. It was one of the days she worked from home, and ever since she had gotten back from her road trip, her mother had been stopping by with great regularity. Today's excuse for being here seemed to be some sort of...um...

"What am I looking at, Mom?"

Sighing dramatically, Irene Mackie stepped into the office and posed–again–next to Grace's desk. "Do you see it now?"

"Uh..."

With her hands dropping to her side, she yelled, "Well dang it, Grace! I got low-lights put in my hair and got myself this new denim jacket! It couldn't be more obvious!"

Looking a little closer, Grace had to stifle a giggle. "I'm sorry, but...is that jacket...bedazzled?"

Smiling broadly, her mother nodded. "It is! Isn't it fabulous? And you'll never guess where I got it?"

"The thrift store?"

Smile gone, Irene frowned. "No, silly. There's a fun new boutique downtown next to that Asian bistro you like so much. Next time we go there for lunch, we'll have to shop."

"Sounds good." Glancing back at the computer screen, she re-read the email she was typing up and wondered if she needed to scrap it and call the client or if the information she was attaching was self-explanatory.

"Grace, you're not even paying attention! Have you eaten today? You look like a mess." Then she stepped in closer. "It's obvious you haven't showered yet. I understand you're just working from home and not planning on seeing anyone, but really, you need to pay more attention to yourself and your appearance. What if the mailman or a delivery man knocked on the door? Would you really want them to see you like this?"

"Mom, I'm pretty sure no one would be scarred for life because I didn't shower today." She gave a small smile. "And they've seen me looking far worse."

"Grace..."

"And I'm even wearing pants today! So really, everything's good!"

Her mother arched one perfectly shaped brow at her. "It's not polite to sass your mother. Now, why don't you go shower and do your hair and put on some makeup while I make us some lunch?"

Ugh...why did she think being comforted by her family would be a good thing?

She started to scan the email again when her mother called out her name one more time–but with more snap and annoyance than concern. With a huff, Grace stood. "Okay,

okay...I'm just going to send this email and then I'll do it. Sheesh!"

Five minutes later, she had to admit it was a good idea. The shower felt great and some of the tension she was feeling earlier was finally starting to ebb.

"But I'm not telling *her* that. I refuse to let her know she was right," she muttered, rinsing her hair. Yes, Grace loved her mother, and yes, she was incredibly lucky to have parents who cared so much. And really, it wasn't her family she was irritated with. They just happened to be convenient targets. No, the real source of her annoyance was Finn.

Three weeks–three damn weeks–and he didn't even *try* to reach out to her! No matter how many times she reminded herself of their clean break talk, she really thought he would have tossed it aside and called to check on her. Or just to say hello! But no. Any news she had on him, she had gotten from Dave, and that was another whole can of worms she wished she could put back.

Calling him the day after she got home was primarily about clearing her conscience. As she told Finn, she'd never put all her martial arts, kickboxing, and self-defense moves into practical use, so knowing she did the move just right and potentially broke a man's nose, she knew she had to at least try to make it right.

Getting Dave's number hadn't been hard.

Getting Dave *off* the phone had.

Good Lord. From the moment he realized who she was and why she was calling, it was like someone had forbidden him from speaking for weeks and he'd finally been granted the right to talk again! It didn't take long for her to realize just why he irked Finn so much. He was chatty and didn't stay on any one topic for long and was basically hard to keep up with. On top of that, he was kind of a doofus.

Like a major doofus.

Half the stuff that came out of his mouth was nonsense and he had a huge ego. Knowing what she did about him, Grace cut him down pretty quickly, and once she did, she began to put her career skills to good use. It was obvious that underneath the incredibly annoying personality, there was a fairly intelligent man.

Someone just needed to help him focus.

And Grace nominated herself for the job.

Not only because it was what she did for a living and she loved it, but part of her was doing it for Finn. Maybe if he had one less thing to worry about in his life, he would be happier and a little more carefree.

At first, she thought her motives were wrong. By doing it for Finn, was she hoping he'd call and thank her? Okay, maybe. That had been her very first thought. But after a second phone call with Dave, she realized he posed a challenge to her that she hadn't faced in a long time, and it almost excited her. Most of her clients were people who just needed a little help to get polished and maybe build up a little confidence. But Dave Kavanagh was a complete mess who needed to be built from the ground up. And once they started really working together, it became one hundred percent about Dave, and the only mentions of Finn came from Dave.

Although she had a feeling that sometimes he just threw stuff in there for her benefit.

And she appreciated it.

Secretly.

But she was still really annoyed with him–Finn, not Dave. How could he not call and check on her? Or how hard was it just send a quick text to let her know he was thinking of her? There had been many times when Grace picked up her phone and started to call him but always stopped herself. If he wanted a clean break, then he could have one.

Even if it hurt more than she thought it would.

"Grace? Grace, are you out of the shower yet?" her mother called from the other side of the door. "You don't have much here to make lunch with! Do you want to just go out?"

Turning off the water, she reached for a towel and quietly groaned. There was a ton of food in the house, but her mother was not into cooking.

"Give me five minutes to dry off and we'll find something. I've got the ingredients to make some fun salads!"

Because yeah, after her weeklong food binge with Finn, she came home and cried when she stepped on the scale. Healthy eating had been the first thing on her to-do list once she settled back in.

"I don't want a fun salad!" Irene whined. "I was hoping you'd have the makings for some sandwiches!"

Ugh...so not what she needed right now.

Quickly drying off, Grace wrapped her hair up in a towel and threw on her robe before opening the bathroom door. Her mother was practically pacing in the hallway. "Mom, what is going on? It's just lunch. What is the big deal?"

Taking her by the hand, Irene led her to the kitchen and pulled open the refrigerator. "For starters, I'm starving, and you always have something good to snack on. But then I look in here and see all...this! Lettuce! Vegetables! Fruit! Where is the chocolate? Where are the cookies?"

Grace couldn't hide her amusement. "Well, typically, I wouldn't keep chocolate and cookies in the refrigerator. Have you checked the pantry?"

Irene's eyes lit up. "Is that where they are?"

"No. I don't have any in the house because I'm trying to eat healthy again," she said, trying to keep herself from laughing at her mother's disappointed expression. "There's more going on than just you wanting junk food, so...spill it." She sat down at her kitchen table and waited.

"Okay, fine." Sitting in the chair beside her, Irene sighed. "I'm worried about you."

Frowning, Grace asked, "Why?"

"Sweetheart, it's been almost a month..."

"A little over three weeks, but...who's counting, right?" she said with a mirthless laugh.

"Anyway, it's been almost a month, and you're just... you're just being normal! How is it possible that you're this okay with everything? I fear you're bottling it all up! You need to talk about what happened and get out some of your anger! Have you been going to the gym? Do you hit one of those punching bags?"

Her heart squeezed a little at the fact that her mother was this concerned for her. Reaching over, Grace took one of her mother's hands in hers. "I'm fine, Mom. Really. I think I'm more relieved than anything that Jared and I aren't together. I didn't realize how unhappy I was until I got home and finally had the opportunity to focus on me for a bit." She sighed. "I hate the way it all happened and how I wasted so much time, but basically, I'm good. I don't need to punch anything or get out my anger. I promise, I'm really okay."

Irene studied her for a long moment before gently clearing her throat. "Well...uh...that's good. I just thought with the whole spectacle Jared made when he got back..."

Oh, yeah. That.

Jared had gotten back to town two days after Grace and

started an immediate campaign to save his job and his image. Her phone rang nonstop from his bosses and their wives and mostly from Jared himself. When she refused to help, he started calling her family to plead his case. Not that it did him any good, but it was a major annoyance to everyone. It stopped after a week and she hadn't really thought of him since.

"I'm just glad he stopped calling," Grace said reassuringly. "He's someone else's problem now, and I can guarantee you he'll mentally exhaust her just like he mentally exhausted me. Good riddance."

But Irene didn't look completely convinced.

"What? Why are you looking at me like that?"

"To be honest, it wasn't really Jared I was thinking about."

That was...shocking. "Oh," Grace said cautiously. "Then...what or who were you referring to?"

"Finn."

Her eyes went wide. "Finn? Why would you...I mean... how did you...uh..." She stopped and sighed. "Okay. Why? Just...why?"

"Grace, when you got home and told us about your trip, I have to admit I was a little dismayed that you opted to drive across the country with a complete stranger rather than flying directly home to us. But the more you talked about the trip, the more I could see you had feelings for this Finn person. Your whole first week home, you brought him up in every conversation and then...nothing." She gave Grace a sympathetic look. "I'll admit I thought it was normal and that you talked about him so much simply because you spent so much time together. But now I have to wonder if..."

"If what?"

Irene paused and seemed to consider her words. "You've been sad and quiet these last few weeks and I have to wonder if part of that is because of Finn." She met Grace's gaze head-on. "Like maybe you had feelings for him."

What good would denying it be?

"I did, Mom." Then she quickly corrected herself. "I do. I really do. But we agreed to just let things go and..." She shrugged. "That's what I'm trying to do."

"Have you spoken to him?"

She shook her head. "Not since the day I flew home."

"Oh, sweetie. I'm sorry."

"Me too."

"I know you just got back, but..."

"But what?"

"Have you thought about taking a little time away for yourself? You know, go someplace tropical or to a spa for a week and just...get a little perspective while you regroup and rejuvenate?"

It did sound like a good idea, but it seemed a little impractical to be taking time off again–which is what she said to her mother.

"Well, it was just a suggestion. And you know if ever want to use the timeshare, it's yours."

"Thanks, Mom. I appreciate it."

They sat in companionable silence for a few minutes before Irene squeezed Grace's hand and then stood. "Well, that decides it."

Grace looked up at her in confusion. "Decides what?"

"We're going out for junk food," she said with a big smile. "Or at least, a somewhat non-healthy lunch. How does Mexican food sound to you? We can eat our weight in chips and salsa!"

Right then, Grace wasn't sure if she should laugh or cry.

She swallowed the lump of emotion clogging her throat and stood. "That sounds like the perfect thing, Mom. I'll be ready in fifteen minutes!" And forcing a smile to her face, she ran off to get dressed.

10

It was a rainy Saturday morning, and Grace stood by the glass doors that led out to her back porch and sipped her coffee. Dressed casually in a pair of yoga pants and a t-shirt, she couldn't help but smile. Today's shirt said, "Sassy Since Birth." It was one of the shirts she purchased at Walmart that fateful night. Never before had she worn t-shirts with sarcastic sayings, and yet she ended up with a small collection of them thanks to their quickie shopping spree.

Finn loved all of them. Every day he made a comment on what the t-shirt of the day said and, if possible, it was one of her favorite memories of their trip. Each and every one of those conversations made her smile.

Meanwhile, nothing else did lately.

With a sigh, she stared out at the rain. Things weren't going well. She felt restless and anxious and–contrary to popular belief–she hadn't slept well since coming home. Sure, that was probably the main cause of every day feeling like an eternity, but more than anything, Grace felt like she needed a change of scenery.

And not just a quick getaway either.

Her home held memories of a life she didn't relate to anymore. Every room was filled with items she purchased with Jared's input. Okay, maybe that was a slight exaggeration, but there were still enough things scattered around the house that brought up negative feelings.

Placing her mug down on the kitchen counter, she said, "Then that's what I have to do today. De-clutter the house."

Two hours later, she had three boxes filled with stuff to take to the local Goodwill. She put them in the garage and stepped back inside and felt...nothing. Still the same old feelings as she looked around. "Now what?" she asked herself.

Then inspiration hit.

She could renovate the place. It was something she talked about before she met Jared, but once they started dating, she forgot about it.

Now she walked around the house and thought about all the possibilities–new paint, new furniture, new window treatments...she could make the place look like something out of a decorating magazine. Only...she felt completely uninspired.

"How is this possible?" she called out to no one. "I am an intelligent woman! I have a great and successful career! Why can't I snap out of this damn funk? Why isn't what I have enough?"

I want Finn.

Yeah, that was what was missing. Grace knew the rest of her life was pretty damn good, but being with Finn brought something out in her she never felt before, and she wanted to feel that way again.

Collapsing on the couch, she knew what she needed to do–had put it off long enough.

She was going to call Finn.

It took several minutes for her to get her courage up to actually hit the call button, and when she did, she let out a long shaky breath and prayed she wasn't making a mistake.

"Hey, you've reached Finn Kavanagh. Leave a message after the beep, and I'll get back to you as soon as possible. Thanks," the message said in Finn's deep, rumbly voice, and Grace practically fumbled to make herself speak.

"Hey, Finn, it's...it's Grace. Grace Mackie." *Ugh, did I really just clarify that?* "Anyway, I was just calling to say hi and see how you were doing, soooo...give me a call if you want. I mean, you don't have to. I'm fine and all. But..."

BEEP!

"Dammit," she muttered and quickly dialed his number again. As soon as she was cued, she spoke again. "Hey, we got cut off. I was just saying if you wanted to call, um...that would be good. I hope you're okay, and you're...uh...you know...good." *How can I possibly be this bad at speaking words?* "I hope you're okay and things are good. Maybe...:

BEEP!

"Son of a bitch!" she cried, angrily swiping her screen and calling again. "It's me again and your phone is stupid because it keeps cutting me off! *Gah!* And I swear to stop saying the word good. All I wanted to do was say a quick hello and...and...you know what? I really thought you would have called by now," she said, calming down. "I really was hoping I would have heard from you. I don't know, maybe you really are glad to be rid of me, but...

BEEP!!

"That is it!" she yelled, tossing the phone away as if it were on fire and called herself every name in the book for being such an incredible dork. With her head back against the cushions, she groaned. "What is wrong with me?"

The list was endless.

She was a great public speaker and was known for her witty and intelligent conversational skills. How was it she couldn't leave one simple voicemail message like a normal human being? If Finn wasn't glad to be rid of her already, listening to her rambling phone messages would be enough to seal the deal. With a sigh, Grace closed her eyes. Maybe it was a sign. Maybe the fact that she couldn't speak or leave a coherent message was enough of a sign to let her know the universe did not want her to be with Finn.

Like ever.

Maybe she was just going to have to deal with the fact that they had one great week together and it was all they were going to have.

And damn if that didn't kill her.

The phone rang, and she let out a loud scream.

Finn's name was on the screen.

Flinging herself across the couch, she reached for the phone. "Hello?" she said breathlessly.

"Hey," he said, his voice was deep and gruff and it made her tummy flip-flop. "Are you okay? I see you called a bunch of times. I didn't even listen to the messages, I just saw the three missed calls and figured something was up."

She almost sagged to the floor in relief. "I need you to promise me something right here, right now."

"Um...o-kay..." he said slowly.

"Erase all the messages without listening to them," she said firmly. "Promise me. Promise me, Finn, that you will just delete them."

He chuckled softly. "Well, now I'm curious."

Groaning, she straightened on the couch before tucking her legs under her. "Trust me, it's awful and you don't want to subject your ears to it."

"Now I'm even *more* curious," he teased.

"Finn..." she whined.

"Okay, okay. I'll delete them. I promise."

"Thank you."

"So...what's going on? How are you?"

And everything in her relaxed. Just the sound of his voice did that for her. "I'm okay." Then she paused. "Yeah, I'm just...I'm okay."

He was quiet for a moment and then she heard a low rumble in his throat. "Yeah. Me too. I'm okay."

There was the same sadness there that she knew she felt, and she wanted to question it but didn't want to sound too desperate or needy.

No matter how much she wanted to.

"How's work?"

"The same," he replied. "Today's the first day off I've had in a while."

"That's a good thing then, right? Business must be good if it's keeping you so busy."

"I guess. But it was more like me trying to distract myself."

And then her heart started to race. "Oh? Why would you need to do that?"

And yes, she was totally fishing in hopes that she was the reason he was working so hard.

"Grace...," he began and then groaned. "Enough about me, what about you? I hear you got a new client."

Laughing, she said, "Yeah. Lucky me. He's a total handful."

"Welcome to my world," he responded, but there was no anger or sarcasm in his tone. "But seriously, you've worked a miracle there. I don't think I've ever seen my brother quite so focused."

"He's a little all over the place, that's for sure. Other

than that, he really just needed someone to talk to him about what it was *he* wanted to do."

"Yeah, that's what he said too."

"I'm hoping he'll have a job soon. He seems really motivated."

"Grace?"

"Hmm?"

"I don't really want to talk about Dave."

"I'm not the one who brought him up," she said lightly. "If you recall, I asked you a question and you refused to answer, so..."

Now it was his turn to groan. "Fine. I've been working my ass off because...I miss you."

Her heart soared! He missed her! Twisting around, Grace stretched out on the couch and then curled up into a ball–practically hugging the phone to her. "I miss you too."

They were both quiet for several minutes. Grace knew she couldn't speak for him, but for her, she was quiet because just saying the words out loud didn't change anything. Finn was still in Atlanta and she was still in Raleigh. Simply admitting what they already knew couldn't change logistics for them.

"Can I come and see you?" she asked quietly when she couldn't stand the silence any longer. "Just for a weekend or something? I've never been to Atlanta–except the day I dropped you off–and I thought maybe you could show me around and find us some tourist attractions like we did on the road."

She heard him sigh. "I don't know if that's a good idea."

And her heart felt like it was breaking all over again. Swallowing hard, she asked, "Why?"

"Do you really want to do the long-distance thing?" he

asked sadly. "A couple of weekends a month and spending most of it traveling?"

"It's a ninety-minute flight, Finn," she reasoned. "That's hardly taking up the weekend."

He sighed again. "You know I won't fly..."

"Then I'll fly to you," she blurted out. "You don't have to come to Raleigh. I'll come to you!"

"Grace, that's not fair. I appreciate what you're trying to do, but..."

Now she was a little less heartbroken and a lot more annoyed. "Do I mean anything to you? Anything at all?"

"You know you do."

"No, Finn. Actually, I don't know! You say you miss me; you say I mean something to you, and yet when faced with ways to try to make something work here, you're unwilling to even try!"

"It's not that easy!" he cried, and she could hear the frustration in his voice. "Grace, I'm just...I'm just being practical, okay? I know myself. I love how you're willing to travel back and forth so we can spend more time together, but...I can't ask that of you!"

"You're not asking," she argued. "I'm volunteering! And why? Because I want to see you, Finn!" She growled to let out some of her annoyance. "We had this amazing week together, and I want to see what it's like to just hang out and spend time with you! And if flying back and forth is what it takes to make that happen, then I'm willing to do it!"

He was quiet for so long that she feared he was going to turn her down or try to talk her out of it, but he didn't. "I'm willing to try too," he finally said.

"Really? You'd fly here?"

"What? No!" he said defensively. "I mean, I'd be willing to try driving it one weekend to see how it is. It's seven hours each way, and if I leave after lunch on a Friday, I can be to you for dinner."

Grace heard him say the words, but there was no real enthusiasm in his voice. And as much as she wanted to just ignore it, she couldn't. "Let's try it out with me coming to you first, okay?"

"Yeah. I'd like that," he replied. "I'd like that a lot."

"Good."

"Any chance you could fly here right now?" he said with a small laugh. "Because I'd really love to see you tonight."

"You have no idea how much I want to, but…"

"But…?"

"I have plans with my family this weekend. It's my dad's birthday, and we're all getting together for dinner tonight and then having a surprise party for him tomorrow. I'm sorry."

"Me too," he said softly. "You have no idea how much I was hoping you'd say yes. I was already planning all the things I would do to you once you got here."

Unable to help herself, she laughed. "Ooh…I like the sound of that. Do tell!"

Finn laughed with her. "First…tell me what you're wearing."

After that, Grace was able to cross something off her naughty bucket list–phone sex.

Phone sex was good and all, but it didn't take the place of the real thing.

Unfortunately, it didn't seem like he was ever going to get to really test that theory any time soon.

The last three weekends had been a bust for their plans. The first weekend Grace was supposed to fly down, she came down with a stomach bug. A week later, she was ready to come down and see him when his shop manager had gotten into an accident and Finn had to cover for him all weekend. The weekend after that, he had volunteered to drive up to Raleigh. The car had been packed and he had full coverage for the shop for the weekend. He made it barely out of the city limits when he had to pull over because he was sick.

Yeah, he was beginning to think Grace was right and the universe was against them. She had shared her theory with him after he had to cancel, and as much as it pained him to admit it, it seemed like the only logical explanation as to why they couldn't seem to get it together.

Now that he was feeling better, he was ready to try again. Hell, he was ready to get in the car right now and take the rest of the week off. It was only Tuesday, but...the thought of getting to see Grace was enough to make him feel okay about leaving the shop in the capable hands of his staff while he was gone. Of course, he'd have to rearrange the schedule and make sure they were all cool with it, but it shouldn't be an issue. He could leave in the morning and have almost all of Wednesday with her and then a four-day weekend. It was perfect! Grabbing his phone, he called her and shared his plan.

"Oh, Finn," she said, disappointment lacing her voice. "That's really sweet of you, but...I can't."

"What? Why? Do you have to work?"

She sighed wearily, and he didn't take it as a good sign.

"Grace?"

"I'm going away for a week," she said after a minute.

"Oh, uh...you didn't mention that when we talked yesterday."

"That's because I just decided on it last night. I...this isn't working. At first it was a little comical, but now it's just sad and...I can't do this anymore. It shouldn't be this hard, you know? It shouldn't be this much work to see each other."

He heard her sniffle and knew tears were streaming down her face, and he wished he was there to wipe them away. Swallowing hard, he asked, "Where are you going?"

"Coronado Beach."

"Wow. Back to California? Really?"

She let out a mirthless laugh. "I know, right?" She paused. "I really love southern California and it's one of my go-to places when I can get away. And since I didn't get my tropical honeymoon trip, I figured I owed this to myself. Not that our trip wasn't great, but..."

"It certainly wasn't tropical," he finished for her.

"Not even a little bit," she said with a small laugh. "My parents have a timeshare right on the beach, and...it's a great spot to get away and clear my head. I think I need that now more than ever."

"I'm so sorry, Grace. For everything."

"Me too," she said sadly. "I guess I should have stuck to our original agreement and had a clean break, huh?"

"No," he countered. "I don't think so. These last few weeks have been amazing. I love talking to you every day and hearing about the things you're doing. Just hearing the sound of your voice makes my day."

Another sniffle. "I feel the same way, but...this is just all too much. I...need to go."

"How long will you be gone?" he asked, afraid to let the conversation end.

"A week, but...that wasn't what I was referring to." Another pause. "I don't think we should talk anymore."

"Don't say that. Please," he begged. "Take the week away to think, but...don't make any decisions right now. Everything else will work out. I know it will. We will be healthy at the same time eventually!" He had hoped to get a laugh out of her, but he didn't.

"Goodbye, Finn Kavanagh. Have a wonderful life," she said softly right before hanging up.

Even though he knew she wasn't there, Finn couldn't seem to let himself hang up. For a solid five minutes, he held the phone to his ear and prayed she'd come back on. When it became clear she wasn't, Finn put the phone down and felt completely numb.

Now what?

Should he call her back?

Give her time to cool off and then call?

Leaning forward, he raked his hands through his hair before resting his elbows on his knees. This so wasn't how he imagined things going. Fifteen minutes ago, he was excited about going to see his girl–confident in the fact that they were going to make this work. And now? Now what did he have? Nothing. Because there was something else he came to realize in the last several weeks.

She was it for him.

Grace Mackie was the missing component of his life.

When she wasn't with him, or at least talking to him daily, he had nothing.

Finn knew he could work twenty-four hours a day, seven days a week, and it wouldn't be enough to distract him from thoughts of her. He could become the most successful auto shop in Atlanta or in the entire state of Georgia, and it wouldn't matter because she wasn't there beside him. Hell, he could win the lottery and have all the money in the world, and it wouldn't matter if he didn't have Grace.

Changing positions, he flopped back against the sofa cushions and placed a hand over the pain in his chest. He was familiar with it—it was the same pain he felt when he watched Grace drive away six weeks ago.

And he had a feeling it was going to be staying with him for a while.

Day turned to night and night turned back into day, and from his spot on the sofa, time lost all meaning. When he didn't show up for work, his shop manager Sean called him, and all Finn told him was he still wasn't feeling well. He thought it was a reasonable excuse and figured he sounded believable since he really wasn't feeling well, but he was wrong.

His brother banging on his front door thirty minutes later was his first clue.

"C'mon, Finn! Open the door!" Dave yelled, pounding loudly against the wood.

"Son of a bitch," he muttered, coming to his feet. Swaying slightly, he managed to make his way to the door, yanking it open. "What?" he asked, turning away and walking back to the sofa.

"Man, I guess you really are still sick."

Finn heard the front door close but didn't bother turning around. Instead, he lay back down on the sofa and reached for the blanket he kept draped over it and tried to cover himself.

"What is going on with you?" Dave asked, concern lacing his voice. "Sean called me because he said you sounded off and was worried." He sat down on the coffee table and stared at Finn. "So, what's up?"

Maybe talking to someone would help.

Even if it was Dave.

"Grace called."

Dave's eyes lit up. "Oh yeah? Is she finally gonna make it here for a visit?"

"No," he said miserably. "She...she broke it off. Said we should have stuck to a clean break."

For a moment, Dave simply stared at him as if he didn't understand what Finn was saying. "Did you guys fight?"

He shook his head.

"Is she seeing someone else?"

He shook his head again.

"Then what the hell happened?"

Finn explained about all the missed opportunities to see each other and how it was clearly a sign this wasn't meant to be.

"That's bullshit!" Dave said earnestly. "I'll admit it does seem like there were a lot of unfortunate circumstances that kept delaying things, but...you can't let her go, Finn!"

He flung an arm over his face to block out the light. "I don't really have a choice. If this is what she wants, I need to respect that."

"Man, I really wish someone would kick you in the face."

Finn lifted his arm slightly and glared at his brother. "Excuse me?"

"You heard me. Someone needs to kick you in the face." He shook his head. "I would do it, but you already look so pitiful that I can't. It would be like kicking a puppy."

"Gee, thanks."

"Don't mention it." Then he reached out and gave Finn a hard shove. "I'm serious, Finn, you can't let this happen! Get in the car and go! Drive to Raleigh! Go after her!"

"I can't," he said weakly, his voice hitching a bit. "She's not there. She said she needed to get away and...and...she left today."

"Where?" Dave demanded. "Where did she go?"

"Coronado Beach."

"Where the hell is that?"

"Southern California."

Dave shoved him again. "Then what are you doing here? Get your ass to California!"

Slowly, Finn sat up. "What's the point, Dave? By the time I get there, she'll be ready to come home, and honestly, I don't think either of us only want to have a road trip relationship. That would be ridiculous."

"Oh, my God," Dave said sarcastically, coming to his feet. "You're even dumber than I am."

Finn glared up at him. "What the hell does that mean?"

"It means it's time for you to stop being so damn cautious! It means you need to make a grand gesture! It means it should be telling you something if *I'm* the guy with all the answers!"

Clearly, he was exhausted because nothing his brother was saying was making sense–which is what he said.

"You cannot be this dense, Finn!" Dave yelled. "Do you want this relationship to be over?"

"No," he murmured.

"Okay, yeah, that wimpy response was completely believable. Let's try this again. Do you want this relationship to be over?"

"The one with Grace or the one with you? Because right now, I'd love to break up with you and have you leave," Finn said with a huff.

Dave shrugged. "Not quite the words of a manly man,

but at least I'm seeing a glimpse of the real you and not this shell of a person you look like right now."

"Dave..."

"Yeah, yeah, yeah. I get it." He reached out and cupped Finn's face roughly in his hands. "Now listen to the words that are coming out of my mouth." He paused. "You need to go after Grace. You need to make a grand gesture to prove to her that you're serious." He paused again. "Are you seriously not seeing where I'm going with this?"

Finn shook his head.

Dave instantly released him with a snort of disgust. "That's it. You're hopeless." He turned and started to walk out of the room.

"Wait!" Finn called out, standing up. "What? What am I missing here, Dave?"

Spinning around, he yelled, "You need to get on a plane and go to California, Finn! More specifically, San Diego. That's probably the closest airport. Jeez! I can't believe you couldn't figure that out for yourself!"

Now that it was out there, neither could he.

Get on a plane and go to Grace.

He chanted that over and over in his mind at least fifty times before he met Dave's face and saw the knowing smirk there. His heart was beating like mad in his chest, and he knew this was exactly what he had to do. Who would have thought his screwup of a brother would be the voice of logic and reason?

"You're a genius, Dave!" he said, walking over and hugging him. When he pulled back, he asked, "What do I do? How do I find out where she is? How do I even book a flight?"

Dave's smile grew. "Tell you what, you go shower and pack, and I'll work on your travel arrangements, okay?"

Never in a million years did he think he'd trust anything to his brother, but right now, he certainly did. "Sounds good." He turned to walk away but quickly stopped. "Dave?"

"Yeah?"

"Thanks, man. You're a lifesaver. Really."

And for the first time since they were kids, Dave blushed. "Go," he said gruffly. "We've got a lot of work to do."

Finn knew that was true, but he had a couple of special requests he needed to convey before they got started. Walking out of the room, he headed to his home office and called out for Dave to follow him. At his desk, he grabbed a notebook and wrote down a list of things Dave was going to have to work out for him. When he handed the paper to him, Finn had no idea if he was asking for too much. "You think you can make all of this happen?"

"Not while you're in the shower, but by the time we get you to the airport? Definitely."

And for the first time in weeks, Finn had hope.

Real hope.

He turned to leave the room and turned around again.

"Dude!" Dave snapped, but he was laughing too. "If you don't get your ass in the shower and start packing, it won't matter what's on this list! Now go!"

"I will, but...I just never thought you'd be the one to step up and help me," he said, his voice somber. "And I don't know how I'll ever be able to repay you."

Dave waved him off. "Consider this my way of repaying you for being such a jerk and a drain for so long."

Finn stepped closer to hug him, but Dave stopped him.

"Although, I should point out–again, might I add–that if it weren't for me borrowing your car, you would have never met Grace. So...you're welcome." And then he gave Finn one of his goofiest smirks and he couldn't help but laugh.

"There's the jerk I know so well..."

"Yup. Now go! I've got your control freak list to get through."

They might not be the closest of siblings, but right now, he considered Dave to be his best friend.

11

It was a little after five and Grace was settled in at the condo and was already taking her first walk on the beach. She would have done it sooner, but she decided to be practical and go grocery shopping first.

"This is my reward for being an adult," she murmured to herself as she stood on the shore and let the waves crash over her feet. It was a little cold and made her jump, but still totally worth it. Looking up at the sky, she closed her eyes and smiled. The sun on her face felt so good and she knew a week of this was exactly what she needed.

Her phone vibrated in her pocket and she frowned. Who would dare interrupt her Zen moment? She had called everyone in her family to let them know she was here safe and sound and no one at work had a reason to call her so...

It vibrated again, and Grace reluctantly pulled it from her pocket.

Finn.

Sighing, she seriously considered not answering. If she was going to work on getting over him and moving forward with her life, the last thing she needed to do was talk to him. She was just about to swipe the screen to answer when the ringing stopped.

And she wasn't sure if she was relieved or sad.

Sliding the phone back into her pocket, she continued to walk along the shore. Five minutes later, the phone began to vibrate again. And when she pulled it out, there was his name again.

"C'mon, Finn. Don't do this to me," she whispered without actually answering the phone. "Don't make this harder than it has to be."

The ringing stopped.

This time she was a little annoyed.

Why would he call twice and not wait for her to answer? Why wouldn't he just leave a message? Why...?

What if he was simply butt-dialing her?

Okay, that would be a reason to be really pissed off. If she was here after escaping to the other side of the country to deal with a broken heart and he was accidentally butt-dialing her, she was going to seriously lose her shit. How dare he torment her like that! It was beyond inconsiderate, and it didn't matter if he didn't realize he was doing it, it was so wrong! And mean! And...and...stupid! Yes, it was mean, wrong and stupid, and if he butt-dialed her again, she was going to answer it on the first ring and yell until he heard her!

Stopping in her tracks, Grace held the phone in her hands and waited.

And waited.

And waited.

Dammit! Now she was really pissed! How dare he not butt-dial her a third time so she could give him a piece of her mind! Of all the rude and inconsiderate things to do!

Turning around, she stomped across the sand and back toward her condo. Once she was inside and away from witnesses, she was going to call Finn Kavanagh and tell him what a colossal jerk he was! Yes, that's what she was going to do! Call him, yell, and then hang up and delete his number from her phone forever!

Muttering the entire time she walked, Grace caught more than a few curious glances being thrown her way but she didn't have the strength to care. Once she was up the stairs and on the sidewalk, she quickly brushed the sand off her feet and slid her flip flops back on. There was a street she had to cross, and at this time of day, there seemed to be more traffic than usual, and having to wait simply added to her ire. In a perfect world, she could have just continued to storm the entire way to the condo.

The condo complex was large and looked more like a giant hotel than the kind of condos you found back home, but her parents' unit was on the sixth floor and faced the beach.

"Just more time to gather my words," she said to herself when she was finally able to cross the street. Through the courtyard and pool area, Grace made her way past the other residents and smiled when she had to and even waved to a few people, but she never stopped moving. With every step, her annoyance grew, and all she could think was how it wasn't fair for Finn to break into her thoughts like this when it was only her first day here! This was her reprieve! Her escape! And dammit, it wasn't too much to ask to have one day—one lousy, single day—to start to heal her broken heart!

Stepping into the elevator with a mild curse, she slammed the number six key and was thankful for a few moments to herself. Looking down at the phone clutched in her hand, she almost willed it to ring again so she could finally let loose all the thoughts swirling in her head.

But then something occurred to her.

What exactly was she going to say? Other than being pissed that he butt-dialed her, what else could she possibly say? How smart was it for her to call him right now? If getting over Finn and doing the whole clean break thing they should've done weeks ago was what she needed to do, wouldn't calling him be counterproductive?

When the doors slid open on her floor, Grace felt a sense of loss. To call Finn or not to call Finn? Had she just walked off the beach for nothing?

"Welp, I'm here. Might as well go inside," she said, unlocking the door and walking into the condo. She immediately went to the kitchen and grabbed a bottle of water before walking out onto the balcony and staring out at the scenery. The sky was so blue, and the beach looked just as beautiful from up here as it had while she was walking it. "Maybe I'll try again later."

Leaning on the balcony rail, she sighed and wondered if it was too early to call for Chinese takeout.

"I'm an adult and I can eat when I want," she said with a pout. "Too bad bakeries don't deliver. I really should have bought those brownies I saw earlier. Stupid healthy eating."

"Grace Mackie!"

Straightening, she looked around and thought for sure she was hearing things. It was a bit noisy up here and it was possible that she just thought she heard her name being called. And really, who around here would be shouting her name?

"Grace!"

Looking down at the street, she saw people walking, cars driving by, but...nothing really stood out to her.

Then her phone rang. She had placed it on the counter in the kitchen and she ran to get it.

Finn.

"That can't be a coincidence, can it?" she whispered, almost afraid to answer it. But she did reach for it and quickly swiped the screen. "Hello?"

"Grace Mackie," he said, breathless and his voice a little hoarse, "could you please, for the love of it, tell the security staff down here by the pool that I know you and I can come up?"

"What?" she cried. "What are you talking about?"

He let out a long breath. "I am downstairs, and because I'm not a resident, I can't get in. So, can you please tell them it's all right?"

"Finn, I'm not at home, and I don't have security, so...I don't know where you are, but..."

"Could you just go back out onto the balcony please!" he begged.

She immediately ran back out and looked down. "Where are you?"

"By the gate next to the pool," he said, and sure enough, there he was. Waving up at her, he said, "Now, can you please wave so this burly guard here beside me knows I'm talking to you, and then you can get on the phone with him to confirm all this?"

She waved frantically. "Of course! Of course! Put him on!"

"Ms. Mackie? This is Garrett Holmes with resort security. Do you know this man? This Finn Kavanagh?"

"Yes!" she cried anxiously. "Yes, and it's completely okay for you to send him up!"

"Thank you, ma'am," he said, and before Grace could say anything else, he hung up the phone.

She immediately sprang into action and began to look around frantically. All of her anger toward him from a few moments ago was gone. If he was here, that was a sign, right? A good one! Finally!

The place was clean, she looked a little like a windblown mess but knew she had one very important thing to do before Finn was at her door. Running around, she found what she needed and had barely time to finish before there was a knock on the door. Squealing with excitement, she quickly made her way over and pulled the door open.

And was more than a little surprised by the angry look on his face.

It was hard to hold on to the pretense of being annoyed when Grace opened the door and looked so wide-eyed and happy and sexy as hell. Finn glanced at her face and then downward, and that almost made him break into a smile.

Today's shirt was one he had seen before that said, "You Had Me at Tacos," and it reminded him of their time in Albuquerque.

And she wasn't wearing a bra.

Damn her.

His eyes slowly wandered up to meet her curious–and now slightly miffed–gaze. "Grace Mackie, if I've said it once, I've said it a dozen times, you drive me crazy."

Her beautiful blue eyes instantly went wide again. "What? Me?"

Finn didn't wait for an invitation; he took a menacing step forward and kept going until he was inside and slamming the door closed behind him. He dropped his duffel bag on the ground and Grace moved backward until she

bumped into a sofa. "Yeah, you," he said, his voice low and–
he hoped–intimidating.

Then she seemed to come to her senses because she
straightened and crossed her arms over her chest. "I didn't
do anything!" she argued. "So if you've got a problem, that's
all on you."

He took another step forward until they were toe to toe.
"No, it's all on you." Now they were almost nose to nose,
and he had to fight the urge to kiss her.

Grace dropped her arms to her sides as her gaze slowly
met his. They were silent except for some heavy breathing,
and he wondered what she was going to do or say next.

He didn't have to wait long.

"You must have broken several speed laws to get here
this fast. You normally refuse to go over seventy-five miles
per hour on the interstates. So how fast were you going?"

"Five hundred and fifty miles per hour," he replied
calmly. "Give or take."

"What?" she cried, shoving him back a bit. "How...? You
can't...I mean...a car doesn't..."

Now he did let himself smile. "You're right. A car
doesn't go that fast, but then again, I never said I drove
here."

She gasped softly and was practically pressed up
against him now, her soft hands on his chest. "But...you
don't fly. You hate flying. You said you'd never fly again."

Unable to help himself, he reached up and cupped her
face in his hands. "And I probably would have stuck to
that way of thinking for the rest of my life if I'd never met
you."

"I don't understand..."

There were so many things he wanted to say to her, but
he couldn't go another minute without kissing her. In the

blink of an eye, Finn captured her lips with his and kissed her as if his life depended on it.

And right now, it totally did.

Grace was up on her tiptoes and pressed against him from head to toe and it was better than he remembered. His arms banded around her and he knew for certain now that he never wanted to let her go. This was what had been missing from his life. She was what had been missing.

They moved clumsily across the room until they fell onto the sofa, and the feel of her body stretched out on top of him, straddling him, had thoughts of anything but making love to her flying right out of his head. Grace broke the kiss and quickly sat up. He saw her reach for the hem of her t-shirt and he immediately stopped her.

"Don't," he said breathlessly. "Not yet." His hands skimmed up and cupped her breasts, and a slow smile spread across his face. "I kept thinking about what I should've brought with me to try to win you over. Tacos never occurred to me."

Throwing back her head, she laughed hysterically. His hands stayed exactly where they were and she felt glorious in his hands. Gently he squeezed and kneaded her breasts until she stopped laughing and looked down at him. "The only thing you needed to bring was yourself," she said softly. "You have no idea how much it means to me that you did this, Finn. That you conquered your fear so you could get here."

As much as he hated to release her, he did. There was no way they could have a conversation while he toyed with her breasts. "I should have done it sooner," he said gruffly. "I should have done it weeks ago. Hell, I should have done it right after you left to go home that day."

She smiled sadly at him. "We both know you couldn't

have done it then. There was too much you had to do, and we said we weren't going to do that. Clean break."

Reaching up, he placed a finger over her lips. "I never want to hear that phrase ever again. It was wrong to even think it was a good idea in the first place." His hand moved up to caress her cheek and then to anchor in her hair. "I kept thinking it was just a fluke. That what happened between us was just because of the crazy circumstances and that once we went back to our regular lives it would be okay, and I'd be able to move on." He shook his head. "But I can't. I'm in love with you, Grace."

A very satisfied grin crossed her face and he had a feeling she might be a little smug about his confession. Mainly because she had been trying to tell him how she felt while they were making their way home and he refused to believe it could be true.

"I didn't think it was possible," he went on. "Nothing like that had ever happened to me before and...I don't know...it almost seemed too crazy or too good to be true." He gripped her hair a little harder. "You seemed too good to be true–even when you were making me crazy."

Her smile grew.

"You once told me you believed love was more than just having mutual respect for one another. You said it was the kind of thing that makes your heart race every time that person walks into a room. At the time, it sounded unbelievable, but then you called me a month ago and the sound of your voice got my heart racing. Then it was just the thought of you. And when you opened the door just now? I thought I was going to have a heart attack! That's what you do to me."

Grace leaned forward slightly and let her hands rest on his chest. "You've done that for me ever since the night in

Vegas," she admitted. "I walked out of the bathroom and saw you standing by the window and looking down at the Strip, and I couldn't breathe. You were just...you were everything." She paused, and he could see the slight flush to her cheeks. "The timing was so wrong, and I kept telling myself it was crazy to even think of having feelings for anyone, so I blamed it on simple lust. Because you, Finn Kavanagh, are an incredibly sexy man."

He knew he was the one blushing now.

"Like you, it wasn't until I got home that I realized just how wrong I was." Then she started to laugh, and it took her a minute to get serious again. "I mean, you are an incredibly sexy man, but my feelings for you are so much more than just lust." She smiled. "There were several long days where I allowed myself to sit and think about my life, and I came to realize so many things. For starters, I wasn't living the life I wanted. Don't get me wrong–it wasn't like it was bad; it just wasn't what I wanted. I let Jared dictate so much and I went along with it. After spending a week with you, it hit me how there was no laughter in my life. Everything was always so damn serious, but you made me laugh and smile even when you were making me crazy."

He could only chuckle because he remembered all the times he knew he did stuff that annoyed her.

"If it hadn't been for you, I'd still be so lost, Finn. That night at the car rental place, I thought our situation was going to be the worst thing to happen to me, and it turned into the best. The first time you kissed me? It was like..." She let out a long breath. "It was like everything became clear to me. You gave me peace even as we embarked on an adventure. You gave me hope when I thought I'd lost every-thing. But most of all, you made me feel when I had been numb for so long."

She leaned down a little further until her lips were a mere breath away from his. "I know now what I want in my life—for my life. And it's you. You make me so happy, and I feel like you know me better than anyone ever has. And I want a chance to make you happy, Finn. I know we can live without each other—we've proven that. But I want a chance for us to be together and have everything we've ever wanted."

His heart felt so full he was afraid to even breathe.

"You're kind of stealing my thunder here, Grace," he said, smiling against her lips as her forehead rested against his. "I came here to make all these declarations of love and you just blew me away with your words."

"That's okay because you blew me away first," she said, kissing him soundly. And then they were done talking for a while. Grace broke the kiss and sat up to finish what she had started several minutes ago, whipping her t-shirt up and over her head. Finn's hands immediately resumed their earlier position as well, and even though he knew there were still so many things they needed to talk about, he also knew there'd be time.

Later.

―――――

"Oh my God, that's so good."

"You sound surprised."

Grace laughed and reached for a napkin. "I am a little," she admitted. "Every place likes to brag about being the best, but these tacos are clearly the best."

"The scenery's not too bad either."

They were picnicking on the beach and eating tacos, and it was the absolute perfect night. The restaurant they ordered from was only a block from the condo, and rather than dining outdoors there, they opted to head down to the beach. "Now you know why I come here to get away."

"I have to admit, it's better than I imagined," Finn said, reaching for another taco.

"Okay, now you have to tell me how you did on the plane," she said. "I'm so stinking proud of you!"

He chuckled. "I have to admit, I almost passed out about a dozen times between the time I got through security and liftoff."

She patted his thigh. "I'll bet."

"I packed some Dramamine and sipped ginger ale and only ate some pretzels while on the plane, but I distracted myself by watching some TV on my tablet, and really, it was an incredibly smooth flight. Once I settled in and put on my headphones and a movie, I was okay. Plus, it was a direct flight, so that helped."

"I can't even believe you did it!" she said excitedly. "But I'm so happy you had a good experience! I'm sure you'll be even more relaxed for the flight home."

He made a non-committal sound and took a bite of his taco. "So, what did you have planned for the week? Anything?"

"Honestly? No. I just figured I'd come here and sit on the beach and listen to the waves and try to figure out how I was supposed to move on without you." She turned her head and gave him a smile. "Now I'm glad I don't have to."

He grinned. "So that means we're free to do some sight-seeing, right?"

On their road trip, she always brought up that idea, and it was highly amusing to hear the question coming from him. Pretending to consider his question, she tapped her chin thoughtfully before saying, "I suppose. I mean, we do have some free time. Maybe there are some budget-friendly or even free places we can go? After all, this wasn't supposed to be a pleasure trip. What did you have in mind?"

Clearly he was on to her. "You're going to make me work for this a bit, aren't you?"

It wasn't a question.

Finn shrugged. "I've never been here before, but I heard Sea World is here, and people think it's pretty cool."

"Ooh...yes! It's very cool!" she said eagerly. "Actually, there is so much to do here! We can spend several days just walking around and still not see everything, so we'll have to decide on our must-see places! When we get back to the condo, we can go online and check it out and..." She paused. "I think it's only fair to warn you, I did rent a compact car. So we'll probably only want to go to local attractions and not venture too far if we want to be comfortable."

"It's a good thing I planned ahead," he said mildly, popping the last of his meal into his mouth.

"What does that mean?"

"Finish eating and I'll show you."

It was a rather vague response, but now she was too curious to eat. Quickly packing everything up and gathering the trash, Grace ran to the nearest trashcan. When she ran back to Finn, she found him laughing.

"What? What's so funny?"

"You really have no patience, do you?" he asked. "There was no reason to hurry and clean up. You could have finished your dinner."

"I was full," she lied and couldn't help but grin. Pulling Finn to his feet, she said, "C'mon! Now you have to tell me how you planned ahead! What does that even mean?" She was happily dragging him across the sand toward the sidewalk.

"For all you know, I was talking about how I had a list made of the places I wanted to see or the name of a good tour bus company," he teased, but then surprised her by scooping her up in his arms and running the rest of the way.

Grace was giggling happily and when he didn't put her down on the pavement but kept walking with her in his arms, she began to squirm. "You can put me down now," she said, even though she was laughing and still enjoying the whole thing. "I don't mind walking the rest of the way."

"I know you don't, but I really like the feel of you right where you are," he said and then gave her a quick kiss. At the corner, he did stop and put her on her feet but quickly took her hand in his.

They started walking past the condo and she tugged on his hand. "Wait, where are we going?"

"You'll see," he said vaguely, but he had a huge smile on his face.

This was something Grace knew she'd never grow tired of–seeing Finn look so happy and relaxed. So much of their trip had been spent with him being uptight, but she knew that was largely because of the stress he was under. Having spent time talking with him over the last several weeks, she felt like this was closer to who he really was, and she was glad to see it firsthand.

A block later, they were in a convenience store parking lot.

"I'm confused," she said, glancing around. "Did you want to get a map, or did you forget to pack something?"

Finn continued walking and stopped behind a red convertible. He released her hand and seemed to admire the car. Grace had to admit that it was a beautiful car. Definitely a classic–probably from the sixties. She stepped in closer and followed him around the car. "Have you ever worked on a car like this?"

He nodded. "Several. I have a friend who lives out this way who is a collector."

"Really? Wow! Are you going to stop and see him while you're here?"

"Already have," he said casually.

Grace stopped and frowned. "Already? When?"

"He picked me up from the airport," he replied, stopping next to the passenger side door. Opening it, he smiled at her. "In this car. Care to go for a ride?"

Her hands flew to her mouth as she gasped. "Are you serious? This is...you mean you borrowed...?"

Laughing, Finn nodded and reached for her hand and tugged her to him. "I remember someone talking about taking a road trip in a convertible and thought you might enjoy this. We might not be driving cross-country in it, but I thought it would be a great way to drive up and down the coast and maybe watch a sunset or two in it."

It was all too much. She launched herself into his arms and completely wrapped herself around him. "You are amazing, Finn Kavanagh, you know that, right?"

He kissed her and smiled. "I don't know if I'd say amazing, but I do okay." He placed her in the car and shut the door before jogging around to the driver's side and joining her.

Starting the engine, Finn got a look of total bliss on his face. No doubt as a car guy, getting to drive something like this was pretty cool. Resting an arm across the seat, he turned his head and smiled. "What do you think?"

"This is so freaking cool! I've never driven in anything

like this before!" She paused and gave him a sly smile. "Can I ask you something?"

He chuckled. "That's my girl. Sure. What's up?"

"Why did you park it down here? You know there's a parking garage at the resort, right?"

"They wouldn't let me park there since I wasn't a resident or a guest, and I didn't want to start our visit out with me asking you to meet me down in the lobby to get a parking pass." He shrugged. "So I left it here."

"You're lucky it's still here. I imagine a car like this is every man's dream and probably high on the list of car thieves."

"Damn, I didn't think about that. I guess I am lucky!" he laughed, then he took one of her hands in his and kissed it. "But then again, I already knew that. Especially now that I have you."

"I feel the same way," she said and felt herself blush. "So, where are we gonna go?" she asked, practically bouncing in her seat.

"Wherever you want. I know it's been a long travel day for each of us, and I know I wouldn't mind making it an early night, but I think a drive up and down the peninsula could be nice. What about you?"

A million different destinations came to mind, but Finn was right. A short drive up and down the coast would be the perfect end to their day.

Well...she had other ideas for how they could end their day back at the condo, but for now, this was pretty nice too.

Finn pulled out of the parking lot and turned out onto the main road. The sky was beautiful shades of pink and blue. There was a great breeze, and the smell of the ocean was spectacular. Grace was on sensory overload and couldn't be happier about it. Finn gently squeezed the hand he was still holding.

"What are you thinking right now?" he asked.

Resting her head back against the cushion, she turned it slightly to look at him. "I'm thinking this has been a great night. The sights and smells are just filling all of my senses and I'm loving it."

His smile grew as he turned back to watch the road. "Yeah, mine too. I don't go to the beach nearly enough. I had almost forgotten how awesome it can be."

"Well, you'll definitely get your fill this week. Stick with me. I love to start and end my day out on the beach."

"Then I'm going to love it too," he said, and he sounded so serene that Grace knew this week wasn't just going to be good for them as a couple, but for Finn as an individual too.

She wanted to ask how his brother was and how work was, but...not now. Now was just about enjoying the moment. Neither spoke for several minutes; they simply enjoyed the ride and took in the views. When Finn turned the car around to head back to the condo, daylight was fading.

"Look at us," she said, smiling over at him. "We're driving off into the sunset."

He kissed her hand again. "Sweetheart, this is just the first of many. I promise."

"I love you, Finn Kavanagh."

Another kiss. "I love you too, Grace Mackie."

EPILOGUE

THREE MONTHS LATER...

"This is ridiculous."

"It's going to be fun."

"No, it's going to be ridiculous."

Grace rolled her eyes and rested her head on Finn's shoulder. "You've been on board with this plan all along. Why are you raining on my parade now?"

"Because I didn't really think you were serious! I mean, out of all the things in the world that we could have done, why would you choose this?"

"Flight 1994 to San Diego will begin boarding shortly," the announcement said over the loudspeaker.

"Too late to back out now," Grace said, feeling smug.

Actually, she was feeling way too happy to be smug.

"Face it, Mr. Kavanagh, you are stuck going on this adventure with me," she said, giving him a loud smacking kiss on the cheek.

"It's a good thing I love you, Mrs. Kavanagh. Otherwise, I might just leave you here and go home."

She knew he was only partially kidding.

Last night, they had gotten married in front of all their

friends and family. It was the wedding Grace had always dreamed of, and it still amazed her how everything fell into place on such short notice.

It had been like that ever since Finn had shown up in Coronado to win her back. It was as if all the planets had finally aligned and things were seemingly always going their way.

Eventually, Finn would see all the benefits to this honeymoon trip. They were flying to San Diego and spending several days at their condo on the beach. From there, they were renting a car and making another cross-country trip–only this time, they had many more stops planned that they didn't hit the last time and a few that they did.

Like Vegas.

Seriously, Grace almost couldn't wait to get back on the High Roller. She had definite plans for that stop.

They were also going to do a helicopter tour of the Grand Canyon while they were in Vegas–something Finn said he always wanted to see.

He just didn't know it was going to happen via helicopter.

No need to freak him out just yet.

After that, they were going to camp out for a night in the Grand Canyon National Park before going to Santa Fe. Next was Denver. The best part was, they didn't have a real schedule to keep, and they could change their route at any time, but they had discussed some places they had never visited before–either of them–and that's how they planned the trip.

Only...Finn didn't think she was serious.

Now he knew.

They balanced each other out–he reeled her in when

she got a little too crazy with her ideas and trip planning, and she made him break out of his comfort zone. They were flying first-class to make Finn more comfortable and relaxed about flying and then staying put in one place so he could unwind. Then all bets were off for several days as they tried to get in as many miles as they could and see everything they wanted to see.

"You know you're going to have a great time," she encouraged. "Have I ever steered you wrong?"

"Wasn't it you who tried to tell me that wasabi wasn't spicy or how it wasn't a big deal to have sushi and Mexican at the same meal?"

"Okay, fine. I'll admit that was an unfortunate evening, but other than that, my track record is pretty darn good. Some might say impressive."

Beside her, he laughed softly. "I admit no such thing. You are a nuisance when left to your own devices, and every once in a while, you need to be reminded that every day doesn't have to be an adventure."

"Oh, I totally agree. Not every day. You know I love curling up on the couch with you after dinner and watching TV or reading a good book."

He nodded. "I also know you are prone to wanting to move furniture or start painting walls at nine o'clock at night too."

"That one only started when I moved in with you."

"You said you liked my house."

"I did! I mean, I do! I just needed to put my own stamp on the place, too, Finn." The house was quite spectacular but very masculine. "I needed to girl up the place."

"Just promise you'll ease up on the pink from now on."

"One pink pillow in the bedroom and you're complaining?"

"That's how it starts! One pillow. Next it will be an accent wall or a comforter...before you know it, our room will look like a cotton candy machine threw up in there!" He was teasing and laughing a bit, but she knew him well enough to realize he had a genuine fear of her decorating skills.

"Fine. No more pink." She paused. "For now."

"For now? What do you mean–for now?"

"I'm just saying...if we have kids and one of them is a girl, we might want to have some pink, that's all." He shifted so Grace had no choice but to lift her head. "What? Why are you looking at me like that?"

"It's just...we haven't really talked about that. Kids. I mean, we talked about wanting to start a family, but...that was it."

She didn't know what the difference was or what was the big deal, but...

"Do you want to talk about that right now? All because of a pink pillow?"

He rolled his eyes. "No, not because of a pink pillow. I'm just curious if you've thought about it–kids. Babies. What you'd like to have. Or when."

Ah. Now she got it.

"Well, if I'm totally honest, I would love to have a girl first. I want to do the dresses and the dolls and dance classes and all the frills that go with it," she said wistfully.

"You know she could prefer sports or working on cars."

She shot him a sour look. "She could. But that doesn't mean she can't try my stuff too."

Finn made a non-committal sound.

"I supposed you'd like a boy first."

"I'd like whatever we have first," he said. "Boy or girl, it doesn't matter. As long as they're part you and part me, we can't go wrong." Then he started to chuckle.

"What? Now what's so funny?"

"I was just envisioning a little version of you. No doubt she'd be a handful and make me crazy with a million questions and ideas and activities."

"Flight 1994, we'd like to welcome our first-class passengers aboard!"

They stood and made their way to the podium. Finn handed the agent his ticket to be scanned and then Grace did the same. When they were on the jetway, she took his hand in hers. "And you'd love every minute of it."

Nodding, he pulled her in close and stopped to kiss her soundly. "Just like I love every minute of my time with you." They made their way toward the plane. "Now come on. Our adventure awaits."

And that was the thing—every day was going to be an adventure and she couldn't wait to experience it all.

AND NOW FOR A PREVIEW OF

WRONG TURN

WRONG TURN

"So...WHAT's new in the history world?"

Chelsea Cooper fought the urge to roll her eyes.

Hard.

Taking a sip of her wine, she glanced over at the person responsible for quite possibly the dumbest question ever.

Drew Russo.

Sadly, *his* best friend and *her* best friend were dating. That meant they were forced to hang out together. And even worse, the way their particular group of friends was, it meant they hung out together a lot.

As in...far more frequently than Chelsea would like.

She had meant to turn to the right after she got her wine and head toward the dartboards, but instead, she'd gone the wrong way and ended up here.

With Drew.

He gave her an easy smile before taking a sip of his beer.

"There's nothing *new* in history," she replied primly. "History is history. As in it's in the past."

Nodding, Drew moved in closer. "Depends on how you look at it, doesn't it?"

Is he insane or just plain clueless?

"Actually, no. That's not the case at all. History is the study of *past* events, Drew. And last I checked, there haven't been any new findings in..." Dare she say it? "The history world."

Now she fought the urge to shudder.

Leaning even closer – like seriously infringing on her personal space – he said, "Well, the past could be anything that happened before right this minute. Me walking over and asking you that question is technically in the past, right?"

For a moment, all Chelsea could do was sputter and try to come up with a witty comeback.

Or at least an intelligent one.

Instead, all she could say was, "Why are you like this?"

"Like what?" His grin never faltered.

Glancing around, she prayed someone would catch her eye and come and save her from another pointless conversation. They ended up in this position most weekends. It was almost as if Drew would seek her out with the sole purpose of aggravating her.

And every weekend, he succeeded.

"Isn't there someone else you'd rather talk to? One of the guys, maybe?"

Bumping her shoulder gently, he replied, "I can talk to them anytime. But you? You I only get to catch up with on Fridays. Besides, I was just curious about what you do. You're always talking about these books you narrate, so I just thought I'd ask. Excuse me for trying to be sociable."

"No one said you weren't sociable..."

"Except you."

The groan was out before she could stop it. "I never said that."

"But you implied it."

This was getting them nowhere.

Fast.

"Okay, let's start over, okay?"

He nodded.

"I just got a call to narrate a book on the Civil War and..."

"Didn't you narrate that one already?"

"There's more than one book on the Civil War."

Shrugging, he said, "Go on."

"Anyway, the original narrator came down with the flu and they're on a tight schedule, so they asked me to come in and do it. So I'll go into the studio on Monday and I only have three days to get it done. That's with all the edits and everything."

"You do the editing too? Wow!"

"No," she said patiently. "I don't do the edits. There's a very talented group of people who handle that. I'm simply the one reading the book."

"And it takes three days? Seriously? Are you only reading like an hour a day or something?"

As much as she wanted to be annoyed with him, she couldn't. Most people had no idea what went into audiobook narration and were full of questions.

It was just Drew who irritated her.

Not his questions.

Forcing a smile, Chelsea explained the process to him just like she'd explained to dozens of people over the years. "Basically, on average, it is a 2:1 ratio. So if it's a ten-hour book, it takes around twenty hours to narrate it. Remember, that includes errors, swallows, background sounds, stopping, starting, etc., so it is for sure a marathon to perform."

Thankfully, he didn't interrupt and seemed to be

genuinely interested in what she was saying. Once she was done, she figured he'd move on and talk to someone else.

But he didn't.

"You must really enjoy history then."

"Why?"

"Because it seems like that's all you narrate," he replied. "I'll admit, I enjoyed studying history in school. I always aced those classes because it fascinated me how far we've come and yet how much we're still the same as some of our ancient ancestors." He took another pull of his beer. "You ever narrate anything on the Egyptians and the pyramids?"

She had to think about that for a minute. "You know, I don't think..."

"Do you think they really built the pyramids themselves or that aliens did it?"

"What?"

"Think about it – how could they move those massive blocks without modern tools? Or toolbelts?" He shook his head. "To do all that work in a loincloth? No thank you."

"I don't think..."

"You'd look really good in the dresses the women wore back then – togas, right?"

Yeah, he's clueless.

A snarky response was on the tip of her tongue when someone came up beside her.

"There you are!" Her best friend Bianca wrapped one arm around her and hugged Chelsea tight before smiling at Drew. "Don't you two look at cozy over here! What are we talking about?"

"How I would look good in the *togas* the Egyptians wore," Chelsea said, praying Bianca would get how that was a completely ridiculous statement.

Bianca studied her. "Hmm...you probably would. They're very forgiving and would hide your hips."

"Wait...what?" Chelsea cried.

"Yeah, a toga would totally be your friend. I like to think I'd be like royalty and have a designer toga that would be more of a mermaid fit," Bianca went on. "Then I'd accessorize with a lot of jewels." She took a sip of her wine before adding, "I'd be totally hot as an Egyptian."

"I'd probably be one of those gladiators," Drew chimed in, smug smile and everything.

"Those were Roman soldiers," Chelsea murmured.

"You ever narrate a book about Gladiators?" he asked.

With no other choice, she did the only thing she could.

Chugged the remainder of her wine before announcing she saw someone she absolutely needed to talk to before quickly making her escape.

Drew watched Chelsea walk away and felt mildly relieved.

He was running out of things to talk about.

Although he would have loved to hear her theory on the whole Egyptians and alien thing.

"You're good," Bianca said with a less than sincere smile.

"Excuse me?"

"Jimmy said you were the go-to guy to keep Chelsea distracted and I didn't really give it much thought. But for the last several weeks, I always see the two of you together so...bravo." She mock-clapped and Drew had to force himself to smile.

"I thought she was your best friend."

"Oh, she is!" she gushed. "But...she really has no idea

how to just relax and…you know…not bore everyone to tears with her work stories. Ugh…if I wanted to talk about history, I would…" She paused. "What am I saying? Why would I want to talk about history? It's over, right?"

He was about to bring up his theory about how history could be from just minutes ago but immediately decided against it.

That would mean talking to Bianca more than he wanted to.

She was nice enough, but…not much going on upstairs. How Jimmy could be so head over heels in love with this woman, he had no idea. All he did know was it was time to move on and find someone else to talk to.

So he pulled a Chelsea because…yeah, he knew her signature move to get rid of him. He chugged the rest of his beer and excused himself.

Clearly Bianca didn't get the similarities because she just smiled and walked away.

Thank God.

Slowly, Drew made his way over to the bar and ordered another beer – in no rush to turn and join the group of friends he was here with or to find anyone new to talk with.

Elbows on the bar, he hung his head and let out a long breath. He was in a serious rut. It was like being stuck in the movie *Groundhog's Day* with Bill Murray – doing the same thing every day and every weekend and it was getting beyond monotonous. They went to the same places, drank the same drinks, had the same conversations, and went home.

Only to repeat it all again.

His beer appeared in front of him and Drew thanked the bartender. Reaching into his pocket, he pulled out some cash and threw it on the bar before turning around. So many familiar faces and he didn't have the least bit of interest in what any of them had to say.

Liar.

Yeah, okay, Chelsea was definitely interesting to talk to.

Mainly because she argued everything with him.

Every. Single. Thing.

If he said black, she said white. If he said he enjoyed something, she pointed out why it was pointless. Most of the time it was thoroughly entertaining, but tonight he could tell she was just irritated with him. Most weekends he could have dragged out that kind of conversation for at least an hour. Maybe she was as bored as he was with these gatherings and felt like he did about their little social group.

How ironic would that be? The two people with the least in common, feeling the same way?

With a mirthless laugh, Drew lifted his beer to his lips and took a long pull of it.

"There's the man!" His best friend Jimmy walked over and clapped him on the shoulder. "You must be losing your touch. You and Chelsea barely lasted fifteen minutes tonight." Then he laughed. "Are you quick in the sack too?" More laughter and another back clap.

"Conversation and sex aren't the same, dumbass."

"That's exactly what a guy who's a little too quick in bed would say."

Ugh...someday he'll grow up, right?

"Anyway," Drew said, his teeth practically grinding. "Any chance of us doing something remotely fun tonight?"

"What's the matter, quickdraw? Not enjoying yourself?"

Drew mentally counted to ten while he took another drink. Lowering the bottle, he glared at Jimmy. "Seriously, this bar is just...we're always here! Why can't we find someplace else to go? We used to do some fun shit before you started dating Bianca."

"Hey!" Jimmy snapped. "You got a problem with my girl?"

"Did I say I did?" he replied wearily. "I'm just saying there are other places to go on a Friday night other than here. Remember when we used to go to the batting range? Indoor skydiving? To concerts? Any of this ringing any bells?"

Beside him, Jimmy leaned against the bar. "Yeah, yeah, yeah...we did all that and it was great, now we're doing something new."

"New? Dude, we've been doing this for months now. Months! That's hardly new."

"Oh, so you got any better ideas?"

"Yeah, dozens of them!"

Jimmy huffed but didn't comment.

"There are other bars, and we could do one of those crawls where we hit a bunch of them downtown, or maybe try the new cigar bar that opened up last month."

"Bianca's not going to smoke cigars."

"Maybe for one Friday night you don't go out with her."

"I knew you had a problem with her!"

Groaning, Drew twisted and placed his beer on the bar before facing his friend. "Look, I get you're all in love and all that crap, but you're not joined at the hip. Once in a while, it's okay to go out without each other." He paused. "For all you know, she might enjoy a girl's night out!"

"She does!" Jimmy argued. "Once a month the girls go out – just them."

"Seriously? Then why aren't we going out – just the guys?"

Shrugging, Jimmy looked away.

It didn't take a genius to know what that meant.

Bianca didn't want him going out with the guys.

Snorting with disgust, he muttered, "You are pathetic and completely whipped."

"Jealous?"

If he had been drinking, he would have choked on it. "Jealous? Of what? Letting some woman lead me around by the balls and tell me when I can and can't go out? Um...no. Trust me." Placing a hand over his crotch, he grinned. "These are all mine and I go where I want and when."

"Do you? Because I know where you are almost all the damn time, buddy. And it's pretty much wherever I am." Then he laughed. "Looks like I'm the one leading you around by the balls."

Drew snorted again. "Dude, that doesn't make either of us look or sound good." When he went to reach for his beer, he reconsidered and pushed away from the bar. "I'm outta here."

"Why?"

"I'm just not feeling it tonight. If I'm going to be this bored, I'd rather be in my own damn house."

"Drew, come on. We're just joking around!"

But he wasn't listening. "I'll talk to you later." And with a short wave, he turned and made his way to the door and out onto the sidewalk.

Knowing damn well he'd be back here again next week.

PRE-ORDER YOUR COPY OF
WRONG TURN
Coming May 2020
https://geni.us/RoadTrip-WrongTurn

ALSO BY SAMANTHA CHASE

The Enchanted Bridal Series:

The Wedding Season

Friday Night Brides

The Bridal Squad

Glam Squad & Groomsmen

The Magnolia Sound Series

Sunkissed Days

Remind Me

A Girl Like You

In Case You Didn't Know

All the Befores

And Then One Day

The RoadTripping Series:

Drive Me Crazy

Wrong Turn

Test Drive

Head Over Wheels

The Montgomery Brothers Series:

Wait for Me

Trust in Me

Stay with Me

More of Me

Return to You

Meant for You

I'll Be There

Until There Was Us

Suddenly Mine

A Dash of Christmas

The Shaughnessy Brothers Series:

Made for Us

Love Walks In

Always My Girl

This is Our Song

Sky Full of Stars

Holiday Spice

Tangled Up in You

Band on the Run Series:

One More Kiss

One More Promise

One More Moment

The Christmas Cottage Series:

The Christmas Cottage

Ever After

Standalone Novels

Jordan's Return

Catering to the CEO

In the Eye of the Storm

A Touch of Heaven

Moonlight in Winter Park

Waiting for Midnight

Mistletoe Between Friends

Snowflake Inn

Wildest Dreams (currently unavailable)

Going My Way (currently unavailable)

Going to Be Yours (currently unavailable)

Seeking Forever (currently unavailable)

Made in the USA
San Bernardino, CA
12 May 2020